The Dead
Farmer's Almanac

The Dead Farmer's Almanac

ಊಲ

JIM LARRANAGA

To order additional copies of this book, contact:
Xlibris Corporation
1-888-7-XLIBRIS
www.Xlibris.com
Orders@Xlibris.com

To Jennifer

ACKNOWLEDGMENTS

They say that writing a book is a solitary effort but publishing a book is a collaborative process. That was certainly true in this case. Throughout the writing and rewriting of this manuscript, I received help and encouragemnt from Laurie Rosin, Bill Enderson, David Hale Smith, and Ed Stackler, among others. I greatly appreciate all their comments and would like to acknowledge their impact on this story.

PROLOGUE

November 21, 1970

JOSEPH SIMMONS WAS strapped to a wooden chair with his arms behind his back, his head dangling just above his lap. A North Vietnamese soldier kicked him in the head again and lifted his chin up with an AK-47.

"Shaman? Rainman?" he said in perfectly muttered English.

Simmons had trouble focusing. The wooden shack was dark except for a lantern on the mud floor behind his captor. The roof leaked rain in steady streams down his bare and bloodied back.

The soldier walked around him and pressed the tattoo on his prisoner's forearm. It wasn't anything intricate. At this moment, Simmons wished it were a skull or a snake but it was simply a butterfly with a circle around it.

"You Shaman. You bring rain, huh?" The soldier pinched the tattoo.

"Fuck you," Simmons said.

The soldier kicked him from behind and Simmons rolled over, still tied to the chair, his face planted in the mud. The soldier crouched down. "You should co . . . oper . . . ate."

"You should use smaller words."

The soldier spit on him, stood up, and unlatched the door letting the cool evening breeze fill the shack. Simmons could see across the barracks that a commotion was underway. He could tell the soldier had noticed it as well.

A deep voice shouted into a bullhorn from somewhere in the jungle. "We're Americans. We're here to rescue you. Keep your heads down!"

The soldier flicked the cigarette into the wind and jumped back into the shack. He bolted the door shut and stood in the middle of the small structure with the AK-47 leveled at the door. Either the frightened soldier forgot Simmons was on the floor tied to the chair or he didn't give a shit anymore.

Simmons heard the familiar sound of chopper blades in the distance and then gunfire all around the camp, but this was too little too late. The Vietnamese had moved the American POWs out of camp weeks ago, that much Simmons had picked up from their conversations. The Americans were invading an empty camp.

The soldier spun around to the sound of the gun blasts. In the yellow glow of the lantern, Simmons could see the fear in his dilated pupils. It was as if the soldier knew that at that very instant a round of bullets was heading for his chest and there was nothing he could do about it.

The door of the shack exploded in a spray of wood splinters and the soldier blew into the back wall.

"Stay down, mother fucker!" an American shouted into the broken doorway.

Simmons wasn't sure if the American GI was talking to him or the bloodied North Vietnamese soldier in the corner.

The GI shined a flashlight inside the shack at Simmons. "Name and rank, soldier?"

Simmons wouldn't answer. He listened to the choppers, the Americans yelling, and machine guns muffling their words. He kept wondering, what brought these men here?

The GI bent over. "I'm talking to you, soldier. What unit are you from?"

He lifted Simmons up in the chair and sliced the ropes off his wrists. Simmons stretched his arms out and the GI caught a glimpse of the tattoo that had intrigued the North Vietnamese soldier only seconds before.

The GI raised his weapon. "Joseph Simmons?"

He remained silent and closed his eyes.

"Answer me, son. Are you Joseph Simmons?"

How much longer could he keep running? He finally nodded.

"Ah, damn, I hate to do this to you, man," the GI said. "But you're under arrest."

He reached down, grabbing Simmons by the arm, as if he planned to drag him away, when a round of ammunition ripped through him. Simmons hadn't even heard the gunfire, he just saw the soldier's intestines fly out of his belly and then he collapsed onto the mud floor.

He waited in the darkness for the second round to take him down, too, but it never came. Across the barracks, the confusion and noise continued. He sat on the chair watching the men running in the rain, mowing each other down in flashes of light like lightning bugs glowing in the rain.

Simmons reached for the AK-47 and the American GI's dog tags. He needed a shirt but both of the bodies on the ground had bled into theirs. Simmons stripped the jacket off the American GI and ran out of the shack. Once he determined where the choppers had landed, he ran in the opposite direction across an open field. He could hear the American and Vietnamese voices behind him fading as he sloshed through the rain swollen rice paddies with the AK-47 above his head and the GI's dog tags bouncing around his neck.

How much longer could he keep running?

November 22, 1970

President Richard Nixon sat at the end of conference room table with his hands folded in front of him, as if he were praying. Beyond the lawn outside the White House windows, peaceniks protested the war, dragging their cardboard signs along the gates like a rattle of machine gun fire that made the President cringe.

Across the long table, Craig Strickland, the CIA's Chief of Operations for Southeast Asia, turned another page from his file and waited for the President to look up. He was always slow to respond to his field reports and lately Strickland wondered if Nixon simply didn't care anymore.

"Mr. President, the raid on the POW camp, Son Tay, failed due to a number of uncontrollable factors."

"What factors?" Nixon said. "I thought Operation Popeye had been launched to minimize the uncontrollable. I was told that we were successfully creating the weather over Vietnam."

"We were and we are," Strickland said. "We've extended the monsoon season, rains have been steady in the region surrounding Son Tay. But the Song Con River overflowed and as a result, the NVA moved the POWs before we arrived."

"The river overflowed. Don't you think that information would've been helpful before we sent men in there?"

"Reconnaissance didn't pick up on it," Strickland said. "The CIA had a coordinated effort with the NSA, and I admit, we were stepping all over each other out there."

"How bad was it?"

Strickland turned a page, as if he needed to refresh his memory. "They walked into a camp with over a hundred North Vietnamese waiting for them. Heavy fire everywhere."

"And why had we pursued this suicide mission?" the President asked.

"To rescue our men."

"Don't dodge my question, Mr. Strickland. You of all people should know we've got men hidden in camps all over North Vietnam. Why did we risk more lives to release these POWs? And stop looking at your notes, talk to me!"

Strickland set the file aside and looked up at the President's dark angry eyes and etched lines across his forehead. The man was old enough to be his father and he felt like a young boy sitting across the long table from him. He wiped the sweat off his military crew cut.

"One of the men held captive at Son Tay is important to national security."

"Who is he?"

"Private First Class Joseph Simmons."

"I've never heard of that man."

"Simmons is a scientist that enlisted with Navy," Strickland said. "He's one of the founders of the Weather Program. Five years ago, he was directly involved in President Johnson's Operation Rolling Thunder. Simmons worked with a team of military scientists to develop chemical weapons - Agent Orange to strip the trees of their foliage, and Olive Oil to make the rain and typhoons."

"And you want him back," Nixon said.

"One of the other scientists said that in late 1967 Simmons couldn't take the pressures of war anymore and he snapped. He went AWOL."

"He ran?"

"Yes, and when he did, he ran north instead of toward the coast," Strickland said. "We had concerns that maybe he planned to trade his knowledge of the Weather Program to the Communists. We've had a team looking for him ever since. When we'd heard that Simmons turned up at the Son Tay POW camp last week, we rushed in. That might explain some of the poor planning."

"Joseph Simmons," Nixon said to himself. "Do we have file on him?"

Strickland swallowed hard. "He's the Shaman, Mr. President."

He watched the President's reaction. If Nixon had read his previous field reports, he'd know Simmons had developed a reputation and a nickname in the jungle as the Rainmaker. Certain platoons depended on his expertise to make life miserable for the enemy.

"The Shaman? A traitor?"

"We think so."

The President stood up from the table and walked to the window, inspecting the protestors with his hands behind his back. "If you think I'm holding a press conference to announce this, you're wrong, Mr. Strickland."

"Actually, Mr. President. I'm here to make sure you don't publicize this."

"We have American reporters in Vietnam," Nixon said. "What if the Shaman finds one of them and talks?"

"We'll say he's nut," Strickland said.

"You have to a better job of controlling this," Nixon said, rubbing his hands together, snapping his knuckles.

"Mr. President, I'll say this with the utmost respect: We've helped every administration since Eisenhower keep the Weather Program a secret. After another dozen satellites are launched, the Program will go global. We recognize that the weather is the weapon of the future and we have every intention of protecting it."

The President nodded and mumbled to himself. "What about Simmons? Do we have any idea where he is now?"

"No, but we'll find him." Strickland said. "And when we do, we'll kill him."

CHAPTER ONE

Plant your beans when the moon is light,
You will find this is right,
Plant your potatoes when the moon is dark,
And to this you will hark,
But if you vary from this rule,
You will find you are a fool,
Follow this rule to the end,
And you'll have lots of dough to spend.

May 29, 1999

MICK JACOBSEN MANEUVERED the tractor across the wide expanse of his soybean field, clumps of wet mud spinning off the fat tires, like chocolate cake off a hand mixer. A cool spring wind nipped at his fingers, as if old man winter were exhaling his last dying breath. Mick couldn't remember the last time it felt this cold in May. Cupping his hands for warmth, he studied data bursting onto a computer monitor strapped to the dashboard.

"It's amazing how well this computer works, Troy," the twenty-year-old said into his cellular phone, his voice muffled by a wad of chewing tobacco bulging from his lower lip. On his left, tall prairie grass in a fallow pasture rolled in the wind, like the tide of a great sea. He hoped to plant soybeans in that field this year but so far, the fields were too wet.

"Dad wants you to come back to the house," Troy said. "He thinks it's going to rain."

Mick flipped across the pages of his notebook and looked up at the gray canopy of clouds. "It won't rain today. It'll rain tomorrow."

"Yeah, I know but come in anyway," Troy called back into the phone.

Mick steered the tractor around, admiring the flat countryside, shifting the gears to gain more speed. Theirs was one of the last working farms in Chanhassen, Minnesota. Urban sprawl from Minneapolis, heading west through Edina, Eden Prairie, and now Chanhassen, made it all but impossible for them to make a decent living. Mick thought his new satellite technology with its global positioning system would change all that.

"How much you want to bet I can drive this tractor with nothing but this computer?" Mick asked, flipping a switch on his monitor that showed his entire field as an orange geometric grid.

"Don't do it," Troy said. "You'll smash into a tree."

"There ain't many trees left to hit," he said, looking out at the field beyond their barbed wire fence. Greedy developers had planted a new row of homes that appeared overnight, like chickweed overtaking a garden.

Mick noticed a black van beyond the fence near a wall of pines. He slowed to look at the vehicle. "Are we expecting visitors?"

"No, why?"

Without answering Troy, he jammed the tractor into a higher gear, and pushed on toward home. The black van followed, keeping pace with him across the field. When he slowed, the van slowed, and when he increased his speed, so did the mysterious vehicle.

Mick felt a trickle of nervous sweat rolling down his neck into his flannel shirt. He stuck his arm outside the tractor to catch a breeze, to draw fresh air into the cab, but it had little effect. The air temperature was warming rapidly. Then, without warning, Mick's computer monitor went dead, as if the power had disconnected.

"Shit, something's happening," he shouted into the phone, watching the van weave through the trees.

"Talk to me."

Mick shoved the notebook into the back of the seat, steering with one hand. "I think somebody figured us out. They're here!"

"Where?"

Mick accelerated the tractor, bouncing along the ruts in the field, toward the bridge that crossed Bluff Creek. He wondered what they would do to him. How had they tracked him so quickly? If he could just get home in time to hide his computer files, he might be able to talk his way out of this.

The tractor vibrated loudly when he noticed a blue light piercing through the roof of the cab that struck him in the head with a heavy jolt. He'd touched electric fences before, but this bolt of energy gripped every muscle and bone and shook him, as if he were nothing more than a wet rope.

His arms and legs convulsed, a pool of salty blood flooded his mouth, mixing with the sweet chew under his lip. The black van that had followed him rolled to a stop. In the distance, his brother was screaming over the roar of the tractor engine. The machine picked up speed, as if it were a bull spooked by thunder, racing down the field. Mick lay convulsing on the seat, blinking at blue dots that smeared across his vision as he faded out of consciousness.

The wind whipped hard across the field, rocking the black van that Roy Manning and Craig Strickland used as their mobile office. From the grove of pine, Strickland could no longer see the tractor.

"What do we got?"

Manning hit keys on a laptop and scanned a series of monitors along the back of the van. "Direct hit."

Relieved, Strickland took a deep breath. "Zoom in."

Manning danced his fingers across the keyboard again and the satellite images enlarged. The tractor had submerged in a creek, the engine still running.

From each small monitor, Strickland could see a different angle; the field, the tractor, the creek water rushing across the dead farmer's face. He adjusted his headset before speaking to his team of National Security agents. "This is Unit One. Ladies and gentlemen, Operation Lightning Strike has been a success. Where's my bird?"

A helicopter dropped over the grove of pine and landed along the bluff. Strickland watched the monitors as three of his team members ran to the scene, picking through the wreckage. One of them grabbed a piece of the satellite sensor and tossed it in a plastic bag.

"We have intruders," Manning said, pointing to another monitor.

Strickland could see on several monitors the dead farmer's brother standing in the field screaming. His father was running from the house.

"Abort," Strickland said.

"We don't have the almanac yet," a team member replied through his headset.

"Family is on the way. Abort," Strickland said.

He watched as the two men and one woman climbed back into the chopper empty handed. The aircraft leapt off the field and circled back, rocking the van as it flew overhead and out sight.

Strickland sighed, rubbing his hands through his balding military crew cut. "It's alright, everybody. We're almost there."

Eddy Osland raced his old Chevy Suburban up a long gravel road, slowing only to read an occasional road sign or mailbox. Another vehicle had blazed the same flat trail only moments before, leaving a fog of dust that crept through his dashboard vents like wisps of smoke. Chanhassen had plenty of desolate roads like this one, where any dip or pothole was a welcomed break from monotony. He took a left at a rusted mailbox with the Jacobsen family name stenciled along the side in bright orange paint.

Sitting in his truck, he examined the buildings around the farm. The barn was a faded red with a cedar shake roof that sagged in the middle, like an old horse that had carried too many loads. The brick farmhouse had a thin layer of white paint covering wrinkles of beige and green. Just beyond the fields, were colorful new homes sprouting up like wildflowers. Red flashing lights from an ambulance emerged through the dust.

By age thirty-five, Eddy had covered countless stories of drunk-driving accidents, and domestic disputes gone wrong. Farm accidents were by far the most difficult stories to cover. As a reporter for the Chanhassen *Pioneer Spirit*, Eddy had covered three accidents, which left him with horrifying nightmares. On one occasion, a farmer caught his shirt in a hay baler, and his arm had been ripped completely off. Then there was the time an elderly farmer lost his way in a blizzard and froze to death only twenty yards from his back porch. When a fourteen-year-old girl had been buried alive at the bottom of a grain silo, Eddy sent one of his staff members to cover the story.

There was something about the family bond on a farm-fathers working with sons, mothers teaching daughters-that made accidents like this so tragic, and so difficult to write about. Farming was a hard job that paid the locals so little. He never understood why it had to be so dangerous.

When he had heard the Jacobsen's son had found their son dead in the creek, Eddy tried to think of an excuse not to come. Eddy had two kids of his own, and he knew it would be an awful scene. This was Memorial Day weekend, and as acting publisher and editor of a small newspaper, he was the only staff member available to cover the story. He planned to take a few pictures, gather the facts, and be out of there in ten minutes, twenty minutes tops.

Loading his camera with film, he noticed the WMSP News Team, the Twin Cities' independent television station that competed against the big networks, had already arrived by helicopter. The photographer was shooting footage as the paramedics wheeled the body to the ambulance. The wind was blowing enough from the helicopter to rip the white sheet off the boy's pale face and blue lips. The kid had probably been dead for at least an hour.

Reporter Alex Andrews shouted into his microphone while running alongside the paramedics. The constant blowing of the prairie wind messed his slick, black hair. "A farm accident turns deadly for one area resident. I'll have the complete story tonight at six," he said waving to the photographer. "For Christ's sake, can we try that again?"

Eddy had grown tired of television news because TV reporters like Alex were more concerned about shooting great footage than telling the truth. Eddy was proud of his interest in telling accurate stories, so he had quit working for WMSP news two years before.

Slinging the camera over his shoulder, he stepped out of his truck onto the dirt driveway. No photos of crying family members; that was Alex Andrews's style. Eddy walked across the wet field and peered down at the tractor still resting in the creek.

From the top of a grassy bluff, he snapped aerial shots of the crushed vehicle. The tractor had a ghostly look, like a ship resting on the bottom of the ocean. Zooming in for a photo of water rushing against the windshield, he wondered what happened here. Maybe the young farmer crashed and drowned Eddy thought. On the bank of the creek, next to a tin of chewing tobacco, were rubber gloves. Pharmaceutical wrappers were scattered in the grass, evidence that the paramedics had tried just about everything. Sad way to celebrate Memorial Day, Eddy thought while he climbed back up the grassy embankment.

Near the Jacobsen house, a teenager was sobbing on the porch with an older man, probably the dead kid's father and brother.

Eddy wanted to make this awkward moment quick. Just a few details and he'd let them mourn in private. "Mr. Jacobsen?"

The man stood up from a rocking chair that creaked as if the wooden spindles were about to snap. "The name is Robert. This is my son, Troy," he said, shaking Eddy's hand. It was a firm, confident handshake. Robert's face was ruddy and weathered like the north side of his aging barn. He had his checkered flannel shirt tucked in tightly behind a large silver belt buckle.

"He's the one I was telling you about, dad," Troy said, leaning against the porch railing. He had eyes like a fish, green and glazed without much life to them. The muscular teenager was apparently blind.

Eddy wanted to pick up the pace of the conversation but felt obligated to offer condolences. "I'm sorry about your loss."

"Never should've happened," Robert said, chewing a toothpick.

"I asked Sheriff Barnes to call you," Troy said. "We weren't talking to any other reporters. I'm a big fan of your work."

Eddy stuffed his hands in his coat pockets, keeping them warm. "Is that right?"

"Your undercover stories on WMSP were great," Troy said. His somber mood lifted as he spoke. "Like the time you busted them cops."

Troy reminded Eddy how he had nearly been killed covering a story that had Minneapolis in an uproar. It was almost two years before that he had discovered three renegade Minneapolis cops were accepting bribes in the form of crack cocaine. By the time the story aired with footage of one cop smoking in the back of a squad car, Eddy had received two anonymous death threats.

"Lately I've been covering safer stories, if you know what I mean."

"I think there's something up," Troy said, his face contorting into a series of quick smiles and frowns as he spoke. "As soon as I realized that Mick had crashed, I made my way down the road. I was shouting his name but I got no reaction. Then I heard a helicopter in the field."

Eddy removed a steno pad from his coat pocket. "The WMSP helicopter?"

"No, this was right after the accident."

"It wasn't an emergency medical unit?" Eddy asked.

"That's what I thought. I stood on the hilltop yelling to them and waving my cane. I thought maybe they scooped up Mick and took him to the hospital. I had no idea he was facedown in the creek," Troy said. His watery fish eyes dropped tears that rolled down his face onto the dusty porch.

"I heard Troy screaming so I come running out of the house. I'm the one that found Mick but he was already dead," Robert said, his deep voice cracking.

"You think that helicopter had something to do with his death?" Eddy asked, turning to Troy.

Robert shook his head. "Hell no. Lightning killed my son. He shouldn't have been out in the field on a day like today."

"It wasn't lightning, Dad," Troy said. "I can feel lightning when it hits. This wasn't lightning."

"Tell you what, I'll make a few phone calls and see who was flying the helicopter around here today," Eddy said, looking across the porch into the house at two women comforting each other on the couch. "Is that your wife, Robert?"

"My wife and her sister," he said, looking through the screen door. "They're pretty upset. It's been a tough year so far with the snow and floods this spring, and now this."

"That's why we invested in the satellite system. We were trying to beat Mother Nature," Troy said, pulling a black, dog-eared, spiral-bound notebook from inside his jacket. "Read this. It was Mick's."

Eddy hesitated before reaching for the black notebook. "What is this, a diary?"

"My son ran the farm these past couple of years between semesters at college. He loved raising the crops. He apparently kept notes of what he was doing," Robert said. "I've never seen that notebook until today."

"We were planning to add those notes to a database of field and weather conditions," Troy said. "The notebook was Mick's almanac."

Eddy fanned through the notebook, blocking it from the wind. Inside the almanac were handwritten pages from Mick. He felt uneasy holding a dead man's journal. "What would I find in here?"

"Something strange is going on with the weather, Mr. Osland," Troy said. "A man from the National Weather Service told us about it. He told Mick how to download government data that would make long-range weather forecasting nearly one hundred percent accurate. Mick was killed because of what he recorded in the notebook."

"That's a wagon of horseshit," Robert said. "You two were fooling around with the tractor on an overcast day and he was struck by lightning."

"It's the truth, Dad," Troy said, before grabbing Eddy's arm. "Go to the National Weather Service. Poke around a little."

Eddy stopped paging through the almanac. "I'm not a private investigator."

"But you're a good investigative reporter," Troy said.

Sure, but that was a few years ago before he bought his own newspaper, settled down to have kids. How could he tell Troy that investigative stories were part of his past? "Thanks, but no thanks," he said. Eddy handed the almanac back to Troy.

The teenager refused to take the notebook. "Read it. Watch the weather. No matter how far off the weather is reported on the news, the almanac is always right. The government controls the weather," Troy said. "Turn to today's date. What does it say?"

Eddy thumbed through the almanac reading the dates on the top of the pages. "He recorded here that it would be overcast. The temperature would be cool, in the mid-forties."

Eddy looked up at the sky. The almanac was right.

"But no rain, no lightning. All the local news said it would rain today but look at the next page. Mick said it would rain tomorrow, right?" Troy said, as if he had the almanac memorized.

Eddy turned the page. "Yeah, that's what is says."

"Mick made that forecast at least a month ago."

Troy was right. Eddy noticed another date listed at the bottom of each page. It was the date Mick made his forecasts back in April. "I'll read this and let you know what I think."

Robert spit out his toothpick and slid a cigarette from his shirt pocket. He lit it and gave a big smoke-filled sigh as if he didn't believe any word of it, and led Troy inside the house before the screen door slammed shut. Troy leaned his face against the screen. "Stop by the National Weather Service office here in Chanhassen. Ask for Dr. Kemper. He's the one that helped Mick."

Eddy slid the pen behind his ear and the notebook under his arm. He nodded to the young man with an uneasy feeling. "Thanks for the tip, Troy."

Strickland had moved the van more than a mile up the gravel road while they watched the local authorities pick through the mess.

"What hospital?"

Manning slid the headphones off his head onto the back of his neck. "Fairview."

"Team two follow the body to Fairview," Strickland said into his headset. He watched the reporter step off the porch. "What's he reading? What did the farmer give him?" he asked Manning.

"Looks like a notebook," Manning said, cropping the photo with his mouse and keyboard.

Strickland squinted. "That's the best you can do?"

Manning enlarged it twice. "We're already less than one meter resolution. I can't get any clearer than that," he said, with an irritated sigh.

"He has the almanac," Strickland said. "Pull his file. Who is he?"

Manning focused the lens on the license plate of the Chevy Suburban as he continued typing. Data lit up the screen. "Edward Anthony Osland: a resident of Chanhassen, married with two boys."

Strickland kept watching the reporter on the monitors. "Financials?"

Manning clicked three more keys. "Heavy mortgage debt, carries nine credit cards. Has a loan on a minivan. He owns that piece of shit Chevy."

"Occupation?"

"You're not going to like it."

"Give it to me."

Manning picked up a stale McDonald's French fry and bit into it. "Newspaper publisher."

"We need to cut off all further communication between the reporter and the family," Strickland said, wringing his large hands. "What kind of utilities run to the house?"

He watched Manning display a colorful power-grid on one screen. "Standard set up for a farm: Well water, septic system, electric, and gas. If you give me a few minutes, I can increase the gas level in the house."

Strickland nodded. "Can you increase it enough to blow it up?"

"The house, the barn, you name it. But don't you think you should check with McKnight first?"

Manning said it politely enough but the question bothered Strickland. As a CIA agent, Strickland knew the fastest way to stop the spread of dangerous information was to kill anyone carrying it. And because of his years of experience with the Weather Program in Asia, he'd been assigned temporarily to work with the National Security Agency to help with this mess.

Unlike the CIA, the NSA was more sensitive about violent covert operations on American soil. An explosion and dead bodies would create a mountain of paperwork back at his Virginia office. His young boss on this assignment, Candace McKnight, would surely want a full debriefing. But he felt this was the most expedient method.

Strickland reached for the rubber stress ball that he kept on the dashboard and gave it hard squeeze. "Blow them all up."

Walking around the barn back to the accident site, Eddy read the first two pages of the almanac. On the top of each page was a rhyme, and below was a description of the day's weather. On the bottom of some pages were drawings of insects, birds, and astrological signs.

Sketched on the inside cover of the notebook was a schematic drawing. Mick had shown how he rewired a piece of equipment to download data. But download from where? Eddy would have to ask Troy about that. On the facing page was Dr. Alan Kemper's phone number at the National Weather Service.

To Eddy's recollection, the weather Mick had forecast for the previous week had been accurate. Eddy decided he'd follow the weather for few days to see if Mick's other predictions would come true.

"Ozzie Osland. What do you know? Me covering a story in your neck of the woods," Alex said, his high cheekbones expanding with each smile.

When he spoke, Alex always gave people nicknames as if that somehow endeared him to people. To Eddy, Alex's nicknames were annoying, like a nervous verbal tic. Originally from the East Coast, somewhere between Boston and New York, Alex had one of those harsh accents. He had moved to Minnesota a half dozen years ago to learn how to speak midwestern, to lose his accent. So far, it hadn't worked.

"If you hurry, Alex, you can still get video of the old man weeping on the porch," Eddy said.

"I tried. The old coot won't talk. What did he say to you?" Alex asked. His tie was blowing in the wind and hitting him in the face.

Eddy tucked the almanac under his arm. "Nothing much."

Alex smiled with a well-practiced grin that showed only his best teeth. "You sure about that, Eddy?"

"I'm pretty sure. The family isn't talking."

"Well, I got bigger stories to cover. Stop by sometime. The investigative team could use you. Our ratings are slipping." Alex thumped Eddy on the back before running to the WMSP helicopter.

He thought about Andrews's half-hearted offer. The investigative unit was the WMSP undercover reporting team. Under Eddy's direction, the team had won three Emmy awards and had uncovered several local scandals. He'd never go back.

Eddy's friend, Sheriff Mark Barnes climbed the bluff from the creek bed, panting hard. "So, quite a mess we got here, huh, Ed?" Mark was prying open a tin of chewing tobacco. "Found some chew. Want some?"

Eddy waved the tin away. "No, thanks. Chew has fiberglass in it."

Barnes wheezed as he stuffed his lip. He was a heavy man with a belly that hung over his belt, like a bag of sand. The steep incline made him short of breath. "You really believe that?"

"How else can they cut open your lower lip to dump in all that nicotine?" Eddy asked, pulling a cigar out of his breast pocket. He exhaled the sweet cigar while surveying the endless landscape, the muddy field, and the creek. "I'm trying to cut back on tobacco."

"Don't tell me you're getting healthy on me, Ed."

"It's not like I've taken up jogging. I'm just cutting back on the tobacco."

"Going home for a little lunch?"

"Maybe later."

"How about stopping by? The wife made hotdish."

"Don't want to put you to any trouble," he answered, knowing Mark would eventually wear him down. "Besides, I got a deadline here."

Because Eddy and Mark were neighbors, the two of them spent a lot of time talking about work. Mark would tell Eddy about all the scuttlebutt in town, like who'd been found drunk in their car or who was arrested for shoplifting. Sometimes he would hire Eddy to research a missing person or locate some obscure fact. Eddy's life as a reporter for United Press International, WMSP, and the *Pioneer Spirit* gave him "contacts," as Mark called them. Whenever there was a suspicious event or unusual crime in Chanhassen, Mark called his neighbor.

"How about one plate? She made your favorite tater-tot hotdish," Mark said, rubbing his belly as if thinking about food made him hungrier.

"Sorry, but a deadline is a deadline."

Mark smiled and played with the chew in his mouth like a cow working its cud. "You're one stubborn son of a bitch, you know that?"

Eddy looked down at the wreckage in the creek. "So, what was he doing out with a tractor in the early part of spring? It's too wet to plant crops."

"The boys were horsing around," Mark said. "You know how kids are."

"Then what?" Eddy asked. He picked up a broken piece of cellular phone from the crabgrass.

"He crashed here."

"Troy thinks his brother was murdered. What do you think?"

"I'm not ready to say he wasn't murdered," Mark said. "Mick told Troy he could cross this field using the computer as his navigational device then boom, he's dead."

"There's a computer inside?"

"They call it precision farming," Mark explained, scribbling in his accident report with his chubby fingers. "Somehow the satellite in space tells the farmer how to read his field better. Most of the locals can't afford equipment like that."

Eddy flipped open the almanac and studied the schematic drawing again. It looked like a piece of equipment that could be connected to the computer inside the tractor. He showed the drawing to Mark. "Have you seen one of these laying around?"

"Mark spit and shook his head. "Nope."

"What was the cause of death? A broken neck?"

"The kid was electrocuted," Mark said. His eyes widened, pushing the wrinkles on his forehead up into his hat. "And there aren't any power lines around here."

"Paramedics said it was lightning."

Mark tugged at his double chin. "A guy could think it was lightning, I suppose."

"What do mean?"

"You have to see the body, Ed. Just about every bone was crushed. In an accident like this you'd expect bruises and broken ribs but not crushed bone," Mark blurted as if he had been keeping it a secret.

"So lightning doesn't act this way?"

"I've lived in farm country forty years. I've never seen lightning pulverize a man."

"Could he have been run over by the tractor?"

"No. His body was thrown ten feet from the vehicle," Mark said, unwinding a roll of police tape from his coat pocket.

Eddy held the tape for him and walked down the bluff, looking back across the field. The house was not more than fifty or sixty yards from the top of the hill.

"Was Troy sitting on the porch when this happened?" Eddy asked.

"Yeah, he heard Mick say something was wrong just before he crashed."

Mick must've noticed something, Eddy thought. "What else?"

Mark gnawed his chew and tied the police tape to a stake in the ground. "I have to check my notes. I think he said the satellite signal died, then their cell phones went dead."

"Both phones went dead?"

"Well at least Troy's did, that was the last he heard from Mick."

"And Troy didn't see what happened because he's blind. Is that right?" Eddy asked.

"Yeah."

"Totally blind?"

"Believe me, the only thing this kid sees is black," Mark said emphatically.

Eddy thought about Troy's claims of murder and took a puff from his cigar. The wind was picking up again, blowing wrappers into the creek. The scent of cow manure from the field wafted into his nostrils. He was used to the smell and didn't mind it at all. Would only be a matter of time before the suburbanites complained about it, though.

Mark whispered to him. "Look, I'm recommending an autopsy. Maybe you could stop by and take a look at the body and then do a little background research. What do you think?"

"If it'll help for the story I'm writing, I'll look into it," Eddy said remembering his busy schedule. He was curious about what had happened to Mick but he had a newspaper to run as well. "Troy gave me his brother's almanac."

Mark held the notebook reverently. "I haven't seen an almanac like this since I was a boy. My grandfather used to record the weather in a book like this."

"Troy said his brother was doing long-range weather forecasting with data he downloaded," Eddy said.

"Downloaded from where?"

"I don't know," Eddy said. "I'll have to ask Troy. What do you make of those rhymes on the top of each page?"

Mark laughed, shaking his head. "You sure you grew up in Minnesota? These aren't rhymes, Eddy. These are weather proverbs. Farmers used to rely on them to forecast the weather. Like this one here, 'Frogs croaking in the lagoon means rain will come real soon.' In the old days, the farmers relied on nature to help them plant and harvest crops."

"Sounds like old wives' tales," Eddy said.

"Could be," Mark said, reading the almanac. "But you know, you're right. According to his notes, these forecasts were made weeks ago and they're right on."

Out of nowhere, a flash of blue light burned Eddy's vision just before a fireball erupted out of the field. The shock from a blast sent both men tumbling to mud. Wood, shingles, and pieces of brick came raining down on them, splashing in the creek. Stunned from the explosion, Eddy looked back to see nothing but a broken foundation where the farmhouse stood only moments before.

Mark was unconscious and bleeding from the ears. Eddy grabbed the almanac, pulled himself up, and ran back to his truck. The back window of the Chevy was cracked in a spider web pattern. The wind carried with it a heavy scent of gas. He opened his coat, stuffed the almanac inside his shirt, and reached inside the truck for his cellular phone.

Strickland slid on headphones and listened to the 911 call. He couldn't believe Osland had survived the blast. He motioned for Manning to turn up the volume.

"There's been a terrible explosion!" the reporter shouted.

"Where are you located?" the operator asked.

"Route 19. The ambulance was just here. Send it back!"

Stickland watched Manning type and jump to different angles of the wreckage. The farmhouse was nothing but a hole in the ground. Appliances were scattered across the field.

"What are you doing?" Strickland asked.

Manning continued typing. "Saving these images to relay back to the home office."

"Alright, people the situation has escalated," Strickland said into his headset, glancing down at a printout. "Edward Anthony Osland is a reporter, which makes him a Class One threat. We'll work a zone defense to retrieve the almanac. Unit Two will be stationed at the county morgue. I want Units Three, Four, and Five to settle into the neighborhoods. Manning and I will go to the hospital to retrieve the almanac."

Strickland pumped the stress ball with his right hand and scratched his this thinning military crew cut with the other. He watched Manning and wondered if this young NSA agent was doing this to cover his ass.

CHAPTER TWO

Weatherman says a chance for rain,
Weatherman says a chance for rain,
Weatherman says a chance for rain,
Do the proverbs say the same?

EDDY WOKE UP with a throbbing headache and a tight bandage wrapped around his forehead. Above him was a collection of "Get Well" balloons and his wife's brown eyes. He sat up in the hospital bed but a ringing in his ears forced him to hold his balance on the handrail of the bed.

Ann smiled. "Don't get up. You're supposed to rest."

"What happened? Where's Mark?"

"There was a gas explosion at the farm," Ann said. "Mark's down the hall. He's okay."

Eddy leaned back on the stiff pillow rethinking the events in his mind when his young twin boys, Michael and Matthew, bounded on the bed.

"Daddy! Look, balloons," Matthew said, handing him the string.

Eddy smiled and felt his head again. "Thanks, tiger."

Michael had a handful of crayons and the almanac. "I'm coloring."

Eddy realized his son had already scribbled on the back of the almanac. "Oh, you shouldn't color on that," he said reaching for the notebook.

"No, mine," the three-year-old said, holding it out of his father's reach.

"Would you get that away from him?" Eddy said to his wife.

"What is it? The paramedics found it inside your shirt," Ann said.

"It's an almanac," Eddy said. "Troy Jacobsen gave it to me. Did they say how the house exploded?"

Ann sat closer to him on the bed, adjusting the bandage around his head. "They think it might've been a gas leak. The lightning that killed the farmer might've weakened the gas line to the house. The entire family died in the explosion."

Eddy didn't believe the house could suddenly explode like that. He picked up the almanac and paged through it again, reading Mick's forecasts. "Get a pen and write this information down."

Ann took one of the Crayons the boys had left on the bed and she reached for a piece of paper on the bedside table. "Okay."

"Today, overcast, temperature in the mid-forties but no rain. Tuesday fifty-five degrees, rain in the morning but clearing by mid-afternoon," he said. "Wednesday sixty-three degrees, sunny, with a southwesterly wind at ten miles per hour." He skipped ahead several days and continued. "Sunday fifty-nine degrees with rain beginning exactly at 4:00 PM."

Ann finished scribbling with the Crayon and looked up at him. "And why am I writing this down?"

It was purely a hunch and Eddy wasn't sure if he would be right, but he reached for the remote and turned on the TV. He surfed to the Weather Channel. On the screen was the daily forecast. The meteorologist was still forecasting rain.

Eddy could see out the window beyond Ann that it hadn't rained yet. He showed her the almanac. "So far, the farmer's prediction is right."

She read the page, looked up at the television, and shrugged. "So? A lot of people think they're better than the weatherman on TV."

"Ann, he made that forecast over a month ago," Eddy said, pointing to the date at the bottom of the page.

Ann leafed through the notebook slowly. "Eddy, what are you doing with this?"

"The family gave it to me. I think there's something significant about it."

"What do mean significant?"

"The weather. Just before the explosion, Troy Jacobsen told me his brother had downloaded some data and he told me to watch the weather. I can't help but wonder, what if somebody murdered the family because of what's recorded in this almanac?"

"He was right one day," Ann said. "That doesn't prove there's anything significant here."

"Then we'll watch tomorrow's weather and we'll see."

He saw his wife roll her eyes.

"Don't do this to us again," she said.

"What?"

"You know what. You left TV news and investigative reporting for your family's safety. You love your sons, don't you?" she asked, pointing at the boys coloring on the floor.

"Of course I do but-"

"Two years ago you said you wanted to buy a small suburban paper and live a quiet life."

"And I did. But when an important story comes my way I can't turn my back on it," he said. "I'm a journalist."

"Journalists turn down stories every day," she said. "It's not like you've taken a sacred oath. Besides, you don't know if this family was murdered."

"They were murdered, Ann," he whispered. "I know it."

"Why would somebody murder them because of what's written in an almanac?"

There was knock at the door and Eddy shoved the almanac under his covers. A large man with a crew cut stuck his head in the door.

"Excuse me, Mr. Osland?" the man said, stepping into the doorway. He flashed his ID. "I don't mean to interrupt. I'm Craig Strickland with the National Security Agency. Can you spare a couple of minutes?"

Eddy watched Ann step away from the bed, her eyes darting from the man to Eddy and back again. She grabbed each of their sons and headed for the door.

Eddy sat up and tried to stop her. "Ann, stay. You can hear this."

"I don't want to," she said before closing the door.

Strickland loosened his tie and unbuttoned his coat, as if he intended to be there awhile. "She seems upset."

"When you're the mother of two and your husband nearly dies in a gas explosion, I suppose it shakes the nerves," Eddy said, tightening his legs over the notebook under the covers. "What can I do for you?"

Strickland walked over to the TV mounted in the corner and lowered the volume. "The Weather Channel always puts me to sleep."

Eddy felt uneasy sitting in bed with this large man standing above him. "I'll say it again. What can I do for you?"

"The NSA is assisting the FBI's investigation of the explosion out at the farm."

"Why would the NSA bother?"

"Could be terrorist. You never know," Strickland said. "Did the Jacobsens mention anything to you? Anything unusual?"

There was something about this guy that Eddy didn't like. Maybe it was the expensive tie wrapped around his thick neck. Or, maybe it was the way he just barged into his room and made himself comfortable. Either way, Eddy wasn't going to hand anything over. Not until he did some digging of his own first.

"The Jacobsens were too upset about Mick's death to talk," Eddy said.

"Did they give you anything?"

"Like what?"

"A notebook?"

Eddy tightened his legs under the covers. "Notebook . . . not that I recall."

Strickland sat on the corner of the bed. "You sure? I spoke with the paramedics. They said you had a notebook under your shirt."

"Probably my steno pad. I don't remember." Eddy shifted his legs under the blankets. "I took a hard blow to the head. Everything is still kind of foggy."

Strickland reached for the paper with black Crayon that Ann had used to scribble Mick's forecasts. "Your wife's handwriting? Maybe I should go talk to her."

"She hasn't seen any notebook," Eddy said firmly.

"We're on the same team, Mr. Osland."

"I don't know what you're talking about."

"We're two different sides of the same coin. You work hard to uncover the truth for the American public and I work hard to protect them from the truth. Of course, we go about our business differently. You use a keyboard and I use a gun."

Strickland removed a large pistol from inside his coat. He released the clip holding the bullets and it fell onto the bed. "Bet I'm faster with a gun than you are with a keyboard," he said before scooping up the clip, snapping it in place, and twirling the gun around his finger. He did it a second and third time, as if he were taunting Eddy to reach for the weapon.

"Are you threatening me?" Eddy asked.

"Of course not. You obviously don't have what I'm looking for. Why would I threaten you?"

"Get out of my room."

Strickland smiled, shaking his head. "You know, I used to be young and cocky like you."

"Really? What happened?" Eddy said sarcastically.

"Reality got in the way. My job took over my life. My wife left me. I only found out recently that I'm a grandfather."

"What's your point, Mr. Strickland?"

"You can work too hard, you know," he said. "Listen to your wife. Your family comes first. Give me the notebook."

Eddy realized Strickland had been outside his room listening to everything he and Ann had said. "If I see a notebook, I'll let you know."

Eddy's friend, Mark Barnes, walked into the room. He had a fat lip and a bandage on his chin. His sheriff's uniform was torn with splotches of blood. "Hey, you look worse than I do," he said.

Eddy nodded to him, making deliberate eye contact. "Mark, this is Craig Strickland from the National Security Agency. He's looking for a notebook that might've been out at the farm. We haven't seen any notebooks, have we?"

Without skipping a beat, Mark shook his head. "Nope, not that I recall."

Strickland stood up quickly, flipping a business card onto the blanket. "If you remember anything, I'd sure appreciate a call, Mr. Osland." He opened the door and nodded to Ann and the boys. "It would be a lot easier on everyone if you'd work with us."

Eddy and Ann were up early the next morning fixing breakfast. Eddy was reading the weather section of the paper as he fiddled with the bandage on his forehead. The twins were sprawled out on the floor watching cartoons. When he heard Ann banging pots and pans, he knew she was uneasy about the almanac.

"Sit and eat breakfast, Ann."

She kept herself busy wiping the counter. "I'm not hungry."

"You're upset about the almanac, aren't you?"

"I can't believe that you're considering investigative reporting."

"It's not like I went out looking for trouble," he said. "The story found me."

"Why can't you let it go? Call the agent that was at the hospital, meet with him, and give him what he wants."

"He already threatened me because of this almanac," Eddy said, waving it in the air. "This is a too big of a story to turn my back on."

Ann walked over to him and sat at the table. "But how do you know the family was murdered? Maybe you're wrong."

Eddy looked over her shoulder out the sliding glass door at the red sunrise that leaked onto the horizon. He remembered a childhood phrase, "red sky at morning, sailor take warning." A red sky meant it would probably rain today, just as Mick had forecast. But what if Eddy was wrong? Was it possible that he just wanted to believe he'd stepped into the middle of a big story?

"I have a feeling about this."

She shook her head.

"Mick Jacobsen's autopsy is this morning," Eddy said.

"And you're going?"

"I'll go to the autopsy. If the coroner says Mick was killed by lightning, then I have no reason to believe that the family was murdered," Eddy said. "And I'll assume this almanac is some sort of fluke and I'll hand it over to the authorities."

"But if the coroner says it wasn't lightning?" his wife asked.

Eddy picked up the almanac. "Then I pursue the real story."

He watched Ann adjusting her nightgown, as if a cold breeze had entered the room. She finally nodded in agreement. "If there is a murder here, and if you pursue it, you could be in way over your head."

The Harbor Funeral Home was an old building with red brick and white colonial pillars, just a block off Lake Minnetonka's Excelsior Bay, where Eddy and Mark did most of their weekend fishing. The lake, with its one hundred and ten miles of tangled shoreline, was so large they had never fished the same bay twice.

Eddy stood next to his truck in the parking lot of the funeral home. He could smell the lake, the rotting wood from the docks, and dead fish. He wondered why the autopsy was here at this creepy funeral parlor.

Thoughts of his wife's concerns now filled him with anxiety. Was there really a story here? And if so, was he in way over his head?

Balancing hot coffee and an unlit cigar, he tucked the almanac in his coat and entered the dark building through a side door. The carpet was blood red and the walls covered with ornate mirrors. The parlor smelled of sweet roses, as if the owners were trying to cover up the smell of death with a cheap aerosol spray.

A note taped to one of the mirrors directed Eddy down a small staircase. He could hear Mark's husky voice as he walked down to the basement into a musty hallway of numbered doors. He was uneasy, as if he had entered a sacred pyramid that cursed anyone who entered. He pushed open the first wooden door and saw a naked woman's corpse on a metal table, hooked up to pumps and tubes. Definitely the wrong room.

"Number four, Ed," Mark hollered from down the hall.

Eddy closed the door quietly, as if he were afraid to wake the dead and walked down the hall. He pushed open the door to room number four, blinded by harsh lights.

The coroner and Barnes were across the room drinking coffee and eating pastries. Eddy didn't recognize the short bald man pacing around, snapping bubbles with his gum.

Eddy smiled. "Sorry I'm late. There was a line at the coffee shop."

"Gentlemen, this is Eddy Osland," Mark said.

"Hi, I'm the coroner, Dr. Neal Fischer. I've done preliminary work on the body. I can answer any questions you might have."

Eddy studied the coroner. He was an elderly man with thick glasses and gray in his hair. "Nice to meet you. Do you mind if I ask why we're doing this here?"

Fischer looked over at Mark who had a mouthful of doughnut. "Go ahead," Mark said. "Tell him."

Fischer pushed his glasses up against the bridge of his nose. "I did the official autopsy yesterday at the county morgue. Two men showed up and watched."

Although Eddy had been a journalist for years, he'd covered few murders and so wasn't familiar with autopsy procedure. He wasn't sure what Fischer was driving at. "Were they cops?"

"They flashed badges alright. They asked for a copy of the autopsy report," Fischer said. "I gave them what they wanted."

"Did you track them down, Mark? Who were those men?" Eddy asked, thinking about his run-in with Strickland yesterday at the hospital.

"They left before I could get there, but something weird is going on," Mark said. "I asked Neal to show us the body here, where we could look at it in private. Besides, this is where the family funeral is."

The bald man chewing gum stepped forward, reaching out his hand with a big smile. "Arnie, Arnie Blake. I represent Midwest Farms. We're resellers of farm equipment."

Eddy was puzzled. Why would Midwest Farms send one of their people? "Welcome."

"The Jacobsens were one of my clients. Mick was using our satellite sensor when he was killed," Arnie said. "I feel awful about what happened."

"Yeah, sure," Mark said. He pointed to Fischer to remove the drape from the body.

Eddy watched Mark and Arnie Blake wince at the sight of the naked body before them, each of them trying to conceal his horror. Mark bit into his doughnut, and Blake snapped his gum. Eddy looked down at the bubbles on the rim of his coffee cup. The lifeless body had a grayish hue and lips that had darkened to blue from lack of oxygen. There were several bruises visible along the boy's chest and arms.

"Jesus," Blake said.

Eddy didn't move. He kept staring at the corpse.

"Okay Doc, let's make this quick," Mark said. "Use words we can understand."

Fischer nodded and began examining. "You can see the bruises along the chest. Some of them continue on the back. This is to be expected with a crash of this nature. We found no water in his lungs. I'm sure he didn't drown in the creek."

Blake chimed in nervously, "You know, the satellite sensor wasn't designed for navigation."

"We're aware of that," Mark said.

"You said that Mick might've been trying to cross the field using our satellite sensor. Our system is safe and reliable," Blake said, his voice echoing in the cold, sterile room. "This could've been avoided."

Eddy was annoyed by Blake's presence in the room. "We know why you're here, Mr. Blake. To cover your corporate ass."

"Says who? The Jacobsens had been friends of mine for over ten years," Blake said. "I watched Mick grow up. But, I think the truth must be told, especially if you're writing an article for the paper. The equipment is designed to help farmers read their fields with greater accuracy, not navigation."

"Nobody's blaming your satellite equipment for his death," Eddy said.

Fischer covered the body with the drape and moved to a dry-erase board. He picked up the blue marker. "I visited the crash site yesterday. Maybe it would be helpful if I sketched out what I think happened. Then we can review the body. How does that sound?"

Everyone nodded in appreciation of Fischer's approach. Eddy studied the drawing already on the board. It was an aerial view of the farm with the house to the lower right, a wall of trees along the left, and the creek toward the top, just as he would've drawn it.

"Mick drove the tractor here parallel to the dirt road and in communication with his brother, who was over here. Somewhere around the bluff, he told his brother the satellite feed had stopped. So from this point he could not see where he was headed."

Blake raised his hand. "May I interrupt?"

"I think we'd prefer that you didn't," Fischer said.

"I know why that satellite feed died," Blake said, gnawing his gum.

"You do?" Eddy asked.

Blake blew a large bubble and popped it. "It might've been solar activity. Solar winds affect radio communications and satellites. We tell all our clients the signal may fail at times. That's why Mick wasn't supposed to use the satellite feed for navigation. It's not that reliable. At least not yet."

"How do you know this, Mr. Blake?" Eddy asked.

"It's my job. I sell this stuff, remember? So, put that in your story. Our system is not dangerous. What killed Mick was a solar maximum."

Eddy nearly spit his coffee. "A what?"

"A solar maximum. It's intense solar activity that can affect satellite communications. About every eleven years the sun gives off more intense solar activity. Technically speaking, we're in a solar minimum phase but we do see spikes and surges. Around the office we call them solar maximums," Blake said.

Fischer stopped him. "That might explain why Mick's satellite connection and cellular phone went dead. But it doesn't tell us about the electrical charge that ran through the boy's body."

Eddy was thinking the same thing.

Blake looked confused, wiping his bald head with his sleeve. "What electrical charge? I thought the crash killed him."

"This young man was electrocuted," Fischer said.

"There's not enough power running through that sensor to electrocute a man," Blake said, folding his arms.

"Cool down. He's not saying your system had anything to do with it," Mark said. "The kid was struck by lightning, right, Doc?"

"Not likely," Fischer said. He walked over to the body and removed the drape. "It resembles lightning, but it's not. You can see an entry wound here by his right temple and there's an exit wound here under his left heel."

"What makes you so certain it wasn't lightning?" Eddy asked.

Fischer lifted the boy's right arm. It made both a sloshing and crunching sound, as if pebbles were just under the skin.

"Sweet Jesus," Blake said, turning away. "Poor Mick."

"This is what troubles me. He was definitely electrocuted, but his body took an awful beating. His bones were weakened and became brittle. All of his internal organs burned. He looks like he was cooked in a microwave oven," Fischer said, peeling back a flap of skin from the boy's abdomen.

Mark and Blake turned away. Eddy stared into the fleshy pocket. The large intestine was nothing more than a jellied mass that dripped onto the table when Fischer poked at it.

"That's enough, Doc," Mark said. "We get the picture."

"If it wasn't lightning what was it?" Eddy asked Fischer.

"I have no idea. I put lightning in my report," Fischer said. He removed his gloves and walked across the room to wash his hands. "I felt I had to give those two men who stopped by yesterday some kind of explanation."

"But you're not convinced that it was lightning?" Eddy asked.

"No. Lightning strikes can vary," Fischer said. "But this voltage was way off the charts."

"What about the other bodies?" Eddy asked. "Was it really a gas explosion in that house?"

"Hard to tell," Fischer said. "The bodies were ripped apart pretty good."

Fischer excused himself and wheeled the body into the next room. Eddy looked at his watch, mindful of his story deadline, and approached Blake. "How did you know a solar maximum wiped out the satellite feed on Memorial Day?"

"It's hard not to know," Blake said. "I usually get a dozen phone calls from clients complaining the system is down. Then I make a call to my guy at NASA, and he confirms the solar activity."

"NASA? You know people at NASA?" Eddy asked.

"Yes, NASA monitors the satellite activity for the military," Blake said. "We use military satellites. The manufacturer couldn't afford to send its own satellite into orbit. It's far cheaper to lease time on military satellites."

"The military lets civilians use its equipment?" Mark asked.

"These were spy satellites used during the Cold War. I'm sure they're expensive to maintain, especially with a tight military budget," Blake replied. "If they can sell time and reduce their costs, why shouldn't they? The government makes big money leasing and subletting satellite equipment."

"NASA tells you ahead of time when to expect solar maximum?" Eddy asked.

"We find out after the fact," Blake said, snapping his gum.

Eddy's mind skipped back over the brief conversation he had with Troy Jacobsen just before the explosion. Mick had downloaded data. Eddy showed Arnie the drawing inside the almanac. "Do you recognize this?"

"Sure," he nodded. "That's our satellite sensor."

"And it downloads data?" Eddy asked.

"Right. That's how farmers collect information to read their fields," he said.

"Can it be rewired to download sensitive data off those satellites?" Eddy asked.

Arnie Blake shrugged. "I suppose it's possible. If anyone could rewire a thing like that, it was Mick. He was always tinkering with electronics."

Eddy turned to Mark. "Troy mentioned that he heard a helicopter in their field after the accident. And I didn't see the satellite sensor at the crash site. Then that NSA agent showed up at the hospital and they must've been the ones pressuring Fischer at yesterday's autopsy."

"You're thinking cover-up?" Mark asked.

"Yeah, big time, too," Eddy said. He turned to Arnie Blake. "Can you get me one of those satellite sensors?"

"Sure," he said. "Name the time and place and I'll drop one by."

At the east end of Chanhassen, the old steeple of St. Hubert's Catholic Church was the first landmark visible to settlers stepping off at the village train depot. The Milwaukee and St. Paul railroad put the village of Chanhassen on the map back in the 1850s. The steeple was also the first landmark Eddy noticed each morning, driving through town heading for a refill for his cup of coffee.

As Eddy had been told countless times in the American Legion bar, before St. Hubert became a man of God, he chased more worldly pursuits. During one hunting expedition on a Good Friday, Hubert saw an apparition of a crucifix hovering above a buck's antlers, and from that day forward Hubert picked up his own cross and became a devoted Catholic. Years later, St. Hubert became known as the patron saint of hunters.

Eddy thought about that as he drove down the road, his head still aching from the blast the day before. The locals had plenty of stories, myths they'd clung to, like the weather proverbs in the almanac that sat next to him on the front seat.

Chanhassen, while ordinary, was evolving into a sprawling suburb. The new residents were delighted when Byerly's, an upscale grocery store, moved into town. Byerly's had carpeted floors and murals painted on arched ceilings. The aisles were shorter and, some thought, easier to navigate. Best of all, Byerly's still bagged its customers' groceries.

Inside was Eddy's favorite morning spot, Caribou Coffee. It was a small coffee bar that made gourmet coffees and espressos. Caribou was Minnesota's version of Starbucks, and when it arrived in Chanhassen, the suburbanites knew their town had finally made the map. At the east end of town was the patron saint of hunters, and at the far west end of town was Caribou. This was life on the Minnesota prairie.

"Looks like you got a big cut on your forehead, Eddy," the barrel-chested Melinda said as she delicately sprinkled cinnamon on his foamy latte.

"I was near that explosion yesterday out on the Jacobsen farm."

She handed him the scalding drink and leaned her wide butt against a cabinet. "I heard about that. A lightning strike and then a gas explosion. Wrong place at the wrong time, eh?"

"Thought I'd stop by the National Weather Service to ask some questions."

She nodded and took a sip of her own coffee. "You mean the new building with the big weather ball?"

"Yeah, you know the one."

"Lots of scientists coming and going from there," she said.

"Ever met a Dr. Kemper?" Eddy asked.

"He's a good guy. He comes in once in awhile," she said. "Most of them scientists aren't too friendly."

By the time he reached the National Weather Service building, his drink had cooled enough that he could hold it in one hand and a camera in the other. He kept the almanac tucked safely inside his raincoat, shooting photographs of the large white geodesic sphere just outside town.

The sphere, or the "weather ball" as Melinda at the coffee shop had called it, sat mounted high above the surrounding homes and trees on metal scaffolding. From a distance, the white sphere looked like a gigantic golf ball waiting to be launched down a fairway. Below the scaffolding was the building that housed the National Weather Service Office serving the Minneapolis-St. Paul metropolitan area.

Eddy looked through a window in the front door and saw meteorologists studying weather maps, computer outputs, and colorful radar images on their monitors. He had driven by this building more than a dozen times before and never gave it much thought. He went inside and chatted with the secretary at the front desk before asking to speak with Dr. Alan Kemper.

When Kemper finally came down the hall, Eddy was surprised at how old he looked. He was at least seventy with a stringy white beard and greasy hair. For an old guy he moved effortlessly down the hallway.

"Yes, sir?" Kemper said.

"Eddy Osland. I'm a reporter with the Chanhassen *Pioneer Spirit.* I was wondering if I could ask you a few questions. It's for a story I'm working on."

Kemper looked up at Eddy's bandaged forehead. "What kind of story?"

"It has to do with the lightning out at the Jacobsen farm and the gas explosion," Eddy said. He opened his coat and showed the almanac to him.

Kemper's face twitched slightly and he turned to the secretary. "JoAnn, I'll be busy with Mr. Osland for awhile. We'll be outside at the Doppler tower. I need to check on the equipment." He turned to Eddy. "Come with me, please."

Eddy followed him down the hall and into the central office. Across the quiet room was a collection of computer monitors and television sets. It looked like a command center for the military and seemed too sophisticated for suburban Minnesota. Along the outer edge of the office were cubicles. Besides Kemper, a half-dozen meteorologists worked in silence.

"Look at all this equipment," Eddy said.

"When you work for the federal government you get the best toys," Kemper said with a nervous laugh. "This facility runs twenty-four hours a day, and we rotate shifts. My shift is almost over."

Kemper stopped at his cubicle where he kept stacks of files around his desk, amongst Snickers bars and pop cans. He grabbed his windbreaker and shouted to the other meteorologists in the room. "I'll be out back checking on the Doppler."

Eddy followed him outside and as soon as the door shut, Kemper confided in him. "What the hell happened out at that farm yesterday?"

"I don't know yet. Troy told me to stop by and see you just before he was killed."

"Damn! Follow me and act natural as we talk," Kemper said, leading Eddy across a windswept field to the scaffolding that supported the Doppler radar.

"Troy gave me this almanac," Eddy said, removing the notebook from his raincoat.

Kemper slowed to look at the pages flapping in the wind. "Be careful with that, somebody might be watching. Come, we'll climb out of view up on the tower."

Eddy stared up at the metal structure as the wind blew through his coat. Above him was a steep staircase that zigzagged up the center of the tower. Just looking up gave him a sensation of vertigo. "I'm can't go up there."

"It's the only place we can talk in private," Kemper said. "If you want information, follow me."

The old man scurried up the ladder like a young child climbing into a tree fort.

Eddy stood there looking up. "But I'm afraid of heights."

"I won't talk down there where they can see us."

Eddy looked at the NWS building and then back up at the tower. "Ah, Jesus," he mumbled to himself before stuffing the almanac into his coat pocket and gripping the metal railing.

He climbed methodically behind Kemper so the wind couldn't throw him off balance.

"Don't look down," Kemper said. "Look up."

Eddy turned his head to see the entire flat town of Chanhassen sprawled out in the distance, like a miniature village in a model train set. A gust of wind lifted him and he clung to the bars with white knuckles.

"Hurry up. A storm is coming," Kemper said.

Step by step, Eddy made his way up the ladder without looking at the ground. When he reached the top, he clung tightly to the railing that circled the geodesic dome.

Kemper reached for the almanac inside Eddy's coat. "This is all my fault I'm afraid."

"Mick's death?"

"The entire family's demise," Kemper said, scanning Mick's notations.

"What's this all about?" Eddy asked, still gripping the metal railing, his blond hair blowing in the wind. "Troy said you'd been speaking with Mick about the weather and that Mick had downloaded data from somewhere."

"I met Mick at the café three or four months ago," Kemper said. "He mentioned to me he'd bought new farm equipment and he was asking all kinds of questions about the weather and satellites. I could see his parents' farm was struggling, so I helped him out a little."

"How did you help him out?"

"I gave him information on chaos theory," Kemper said. "And I told him about Chaotica." Eddy knew a little about chaos theory, the science that studied unpredictable events such as the weather. The meteorologists at WMSP used to talk about it a lot. "What's Chaotica?"

"It's an underground society that believes that the government actually controls weather. I gave Mick our literature and told him that if he could tap into the government weather database, he'd have more success with his crops."

Eddy thought about what he'd read in the almanac and what he'd seen on the Weather Channel. "So it's true? The weather is man-made?"

Kemper nodded. "Some of us think the government employs a database of preset weather patterns."

"And Mick downloaded this secret information?"

"I didn't realize he had until I heard the family was killed yesterday. I gave him suggestions on how he might alter the satellite sensor so he could steal data off weather satellites," Kemper said, pointing at the schematic drawing in Mick's almanac. "And then I gave him software to translate encrypted data. In all honesty, I never thought he would actually succeed. I have friends in the underground who've been working on this for years. Mick's the first person to be able to tap into the database. The satellite equipment is crude."

"But it works," Eddy said. "He forecasted rain for today and it feels like rain."

"I never should've done it. I should've kept my mouth shut. They'll be looking for me," Kemper said. "They know that I know."

Eddy nodded. "Somebody from the National Security Agency approached me yesterday looking for the almanac."

"This is dangerous information you have here," Kemper said. "They'll stop at nothing to get this almanac."

"How do you know so much about this?" Eddy asked.

"I've been around awhile. I've done a lot of academic research on chaos theory. I'm a retired university professor working as a volunteer at this NWS facility. I'm kind of a mole, for the underground."

"Tell me about the database of weather patterns."

"It's just a theory," Kemper said. "In the early days, back in the late fifties, the government experimented with chemicals to seed clouds and create rain. By now they've got lasers and satellite technology."

"I was just at Mick's autopsy," Eddy said. "His body was beat up pretty bad, as if he might've been hit by lightning. But the coroner said it couldn't have been."

Kemper scratched his head. "There was no lightning in Chanhassen yesterday. My guess is they used a military weapon, like a laser to kill him."

One of Kemper's co-workers stepped outside the building, yelling to them about an upcoming storm. Eddy looked out onto the horizon and saw dark thunderclouds rolling in from the west. It was a strange feeling to know that the clouds were possibly man-made.

Kemper looked at the almanac and then back up at the sky. "This is amazing. We didn't see this storm coming until two hours ago. We better get down."

Eddy climbed first and Kemper followed. When they reached the ground, he handed back the almanac.

"When I heard about the Jacobsen's yesterday," Kemper said. "I e-mailed a friend of mine from the underground, Joe Simmons. I think he would be very interested in the almanac. Are you going to write about this?"

"I don't know yet," Eddy said. "I think I need to recreate what Mick did. Download the data myself."

"You'll need the software to break into the encrypted data," Kemper said. "And I got that from Simmons and his friends. They're the only ones I know and trust who can help you translate the data. I'll contact him. He could help you validate your claims."

"Thanks, I appreciate that."

Kemper watched the storm pushing toward them. "I'll take an early lunch and meet you in one hour at the Landscape Arboretum. Go there and show this almanac to Dr. Waverly."

Kemper's co-worker called to him again as rain began falling onto the ground around them, just as Mick had forecast in the almanac.

"What are you waiting for?" Kemper asked. "Go!"

CHAPTER THREE

Frogs croaking in the lagoon means rain
will come real soon.

THE MINNESOTA LANDSCAPE Arboretum was cloistered behind a marsh off highway 5 on Chanhassen's west end. Eddy parked his truck, stuffed the almanac in his coat, and jogged through the rain up the brick path to a large building with a gabled roof and a stone face. Before entering the building, he noticed a black van that had followed him on the highway was now cruising slowly through the parking lot. Instinctively, he buttoned his coat over the almanac and entered the building.

Inside, a man with a nametag labeled "Bart" stood by the doorway handing out trail maps and brochures.

"I'm looking for Dr. Waverly," Eddy said. "Where would I find him?"

"She. Dr. Waverly is a woman," the man said, before pointing to a doorway.

Eddy smiled and walked down the hall to a room next to an espresso cart. The tile floor had smudges of dirt and grass, and the window had a small stained-glass flower coated by years of dust. Hanging plants draped over the windowsills, cascading toward the tile floor.

Eddy watched a woman, who looked to be in her late fifties, remove a small tray from a refrigerator that resembled a miniature morgue. Spread across the tray were dead frogs with their arms and legs taped down.

"Excuse me," Eddy said.

She turned and squinted at him, wiping a hand on her blue jeans. "Sorry, the walking tour was postponed because of the rain."

He reached out his hand. "Hi, I'm Eddy Osland, reporter for the Chanhassen *Pioneer Spirit.*"

She set the tray of frogs on her desk but didn't shake his hand. Eddy tried to place her style of dress; she was sort of a hippie with black and silver hair down to her elbows and clogs that added at least two inches to her height.

"Dr. Kemper asked me to stop by," Eddy said. "Did he call you? We were supposed to meet here."

She glanced at a cellular phone on her desk. "I haven't received any calls from Dr. Kemper. What's the nature of this meeting?"

Eddy handed her the almanac and closed the door. "Yesterday the Jacobsen family was murdered because of what's recorded in this notebook."

Craig Strickland took another sip of his coffee as the heavy rain pounded the hood of the van. Manning was already inside the NWS building flashing his ID and talking to the receptionist.

All they wanted to do was ask Kemper a series of standard questions. Why was he speaking with Edward Osland? Had he seen an almanac? They fully expected cooperation, but Strickland noticed Kemper rounding the outside corner of the building.

The old man dragged his coat in one hand and a stack of papers in the other across the parking lot to his car.

"He's leaving from the south side of the building," Strickland said to Manning in his headset.

"I'm on him," Manning replied, bursting out the emergency door.

Strickland watched as Kemper jumped into his Ford Tempo and floored it in reverse, almost running Manning down. The car accelerated across the parking lot, bouncing over speed bumps.

Strickland threw the van in gear, picked up his partner, and continued the chase. "Sit in the back," Strickland said. "I want you tracking him as we drive."

"You got it," Manning said. He buckled himself to the seat in the back and turned on the monitor switches.

Waverly rolled hair over one ear and examined the almanac. Eddy watched for a reaction but her face lacked any discernable expression. Occasionally she looked up at him before turning a page and reading again.

He couldn't stand the silence and decided to break it. "Are you member of Chaotica, Dr. Waverly?"

She looked up slowly. "Who told you that?"

"Dr. Kemper."

"When I was a much younger woman, back in the sixties, I was a founding member of that group. The underground no longer exists."

"Your goal was to prove that the U.S. government controls the weather, right?"

She hesitated. "Yes, that was the goal back then."

"I think I've found what you've been looking for," Eddy said. "A farmer here in town tapped into a government weather database. We think that's how he collected the forecasts in that almanac."

She leaned against the desk and read another page before shaking her head. "Goddamn you," she said.

"What's wrong?"

She cursed him again under her breath as she read Mick's notations and looked out at the rain dripping on her window.

"God!"

"What?" Eddy asked.

"For nearly forty years I've watched people slave over this and get nowhere," she said. "Then you walk in here and hand me this notebook!"

"I'm sorry. Dr. Kemper told me to show it to you."

"He sent you here because he thinks this proves my own theory," she said. "And he might be right."

"What's your theory?"

"I've always thought that the government's weather tampering is having adverse effects on our planet. That's why I'm studying these frogs."

"What happened to them?" Eddy asked.

She poked at one of the dead frogs. "They're born mutated. Some have deformed feet. I've scraped up money for research. But with this almanac we finally have the break we need. That is, if we can convince the skeptics."

"Why wouldn't people believe us? Mick's drawn a picture of the satellite sensor. His notes explain how he rewired it. The forecasts so far seem accurate," Eddy said.

"Except this date here two weeks ago," Waverly said, paging back. "I remember it because it was my nephew's graduation. The official weather forecast for that day was for rain and that's also what this farmer had recorded for that day but it was sunny. I remember it well."

Eddy reached for the almanac. "Mick was wrong on that date?"

"It will create doubts for some people but it doesn't necessarily weaken our case," she said.

"Doesn't the credibility of the almanac rely on how accurate Mick was with it?"

"Within reason," Waverly said. "You see, it's been my belief that the government *manipulates* the weather every day. And it looks like Mick might have tapped into a database of preset weather patterns. However, the beauty of controlling the weather is that the government can change it to suit its immediate needs.

"So, the forecasts you have here won't always be right. They may be extremely accurate but they won't be one hundred percent. If we want credible evidence, we have to download more recent weather data."

"We have to reinvent what Mick did and tap into that database to show the cynics how it's done," Eddy said.

"Yes, I think so," Waverly said.

"Dr. Kemper says we'll need help from a friend of his in the underground."

"Which friend?"

"A man named Joe Simmons."

Waverly laughed. "Simmons? Good luck."

"Why?"

"Joe Simmons was a whiz kid in chaos theory back in the sixties. We were both students of Kemper's at the University of Minnesota. In fact, Simmons was the one who convinced me back then that the government could some day control the weather. He was ahead of his time. These days Simmons is pretty screwed up. He's sort of a recluse."

"He has software that can open the encrypted data."

"Simmons hangs around with a couple of young computer hackers. If he ever decided to be a part of normal society, he could help us. But from what Kemper's told me about him, that would be a pretty big if," she said.

"He already gave Kemper that software once," Eddy said. "That's how Mick cracked into the data."

"And Mick is dead. Simmons is a recluse for a reason, Eddy," she said. "How many people know you have this almanac?"

"A handful."

"Tell me who."

Eddy had to think about it. "My wife, Sheriff Barnes, Arnie Blake, Dr. Kemper, you," he said, adding up the people. "And a man named Strickland from the NSA."

"The NSA?"

"Yeah, but I blew him off," Eddy said. "I told him I didn't have what he was looking for."

She backed away from him. "You're tainted."

"What does that mean?"

He watched her walk to the window, look outside at the trees, and pull the drapes closed. "They're all over you and you don't even know it. This almanac is pretty circumstantial evidence but it's damaging enough. They'll kill you for this. I suggest you leave here right now. Your life is in danger."

Eddy looked at his watch. "Leave? Dr. Kemper will be here any minute."

"The government treats this kind of breach of security very seriously. And the NSA acts quickly."

"But Dr. Kemper-"

"Forget about Dr. Kemper. Don't you see? If we had this information and the NSA didn't know about it, we might be able to prepare a case against the government and live to tell about it," she said. "But if they already know, then we're fucked."

Eddy couldn't believe how she'd suddenly changed her enthusiasm. "Let's see what Dr. Kemper thinks when he arrives. Then he can contact Simmons and we can get to work on this."

She shook her head. "You don't have that kind of time. If you don't hand over that information, you're dead. Your days are numbered, Eddy."

"Not if I can get help from Simmons," Eddy said.

"That's the other problem," she said. "Simmons isn't the kind of person you just pick up the phone and call. He lives on a boat somewhere in the Louisiana bayous. He's a paranoid freak with no permanent address."

"Dr. Kemper sent him an e-mail," Eddy said.

"And once Simmons learns that somebody died trying this, you'll never hear from him," she said.

"Dr. Waverly, are you saying you're not interested in this?" Eddy asked.

"It's not worth losing my life over," she said. "Better evidence will surface someday with better odds for success."

Eddy checked his watch. Kemper was thirty minutes late. "I should go. When Dr. Kemper shows up, ask him to call me."

He handed her a business card, picked up the almanac, and opened the door.

Dr. Waverly slipped the card into her jeans. "Remember what I said. You're tainted. Be very careful. That almanac may be the only reason you're still alive."

Strickland forced the armored van through traffic keeping pace with Kemper's little car. He felt he had an unfair advantage and every few minutes he gave the old man some breathing room. With a SAT tracking device he really didn't need to ride the guy's ass.

"This is Unit One. We are in pursuit of Dr. Alan Kemper, the latest person to be exposed to Edward Osland. Unit Three, I need an update on Osland."

A female agent named Lisa Wentz from Unit Three chimed into his headset. "He's leaving the arboretum now. We think he still has the almanac."

"Who did he meet with?" Strickland asked.

"Dr. Sarah Waverly," Wentz said. "She's a long-time friend of Dr. Kemper's. She has a history of radical war protests back in the sixties. She's a member of Chaotica."

Strickland swerved the van around a slow truck. "What has she done recently?"

"Nothing much," Wentz said. "She's researching reptiles or birds."

"Talk to her, see what she knows," Strickland said. "We'll do a pick and roll. Unit Two cover Osland."

He drove with one hand wrapped tightly on the steering wheel. With his free hand, Strickland pushed buttons on the dashboard display, reading maps of the roads cutting across town. "Roy, would you throw a series of red lights in Dr. Kemper's path? Let's take him out."

"Don't you want to ask him what he discussed with Osland?"

"He sent Osland to Dr. Waverly. I think I already have my answer. Kill Kemper," Strickland said.

Manning hesitated for a long moment and then began typing commands on his keyboard. Strickland watched the Ford Tempo snake around traffic. Kemper slowed for the first red light, he gunned his way through the second, but on the third, his luck ran out. The Ford Tempo broadsided a garbage truck in a blast of flying metal and glass.

Manning leaned back in his swivel chair. "Oh, damn."

Strickland looked in the rearview mirror back at his partner who had his face close to one of the monitors. "How bad?"

Manning increased the satellite image of Kemper's car up the road. "He's toast."

Agent Lisa Wentz went into the arboretum building alone while her two partners waited in the van outside. After getting directions to Dr. Waverly's office, she walked up to the closed door and gave it a knock.

She knocked again and opened the door. A cool breeze passed her as she entered the office. The drapes were flapping against the windows. Agent Wentz ran to the window and looked down to the ground where she saw footprints in the mud outside.

She pressed the button on her headset. "Dr. Waverly is on the run."

Eddy left the arboretum and drove along the back roads watching for the black van. The rain splattered hard and the windshield wiper blades swept across the glass, tossing sheets of water left and right. He saw a woman on horseback, and a man jogging, and wondered if they were from the NSA. Were they everywhere like Dr. Waverly had said?

He looked into the cracked side-mirror and realized the black van that had been in the parking lot was gone, or at least no longer visible. He drove home quickly, speeding by neighborhoods such as Timberwood, The Oaks, and Trotters Ridge.

Turning left at Stone Creek, he slowed letting a flock of Canadian geese cross the street. Before hunting season in Minnesota, geese were like sacred cows, roaming the streets and sidewalks unimpeded by people or traffic. He was in such a hurry to get home, he nearly plowed over the birds.

The Osland house was a two-story colonial sitting high on a ridge, with a good view of the pond in the backyard. Eddy pulled into the garage, turned off the engine, and went inside with the almanac.

"Daddy's home!" Matthew screamed, running across the kitchen to greet his father.

Eddy picked him up and carried him around the house as he closed the blinds over the windows.

Matthew looked at him funny. "Nighttime, Daddy?"

"That's right, let's pretend it's nighttime," he said.

The phone rang and Eddy waited a moment before picking it up. He looked at the caller ID display. Its ID was "unavailable."

"Hello?" he said, holding Matthew on his hip.

"Don't say my name because they're listening to this phone call."

Eddy recognized Dr. Sarah Waverly's voice.

"Turn on the Channel 12 News," she said. "They got to Dr. Kemper. Remember, you're tainted."

He cradled the phone with one ear and reached for the TV remote. "What happened?"

Dr. Waverly hung up without answering and Eddy stood there watching the TV. Alex Andrews from WMSP was on the scene of a traffic accident. A car had broadsided a semi-truck and rescue workers were still trying to pry the body out of the crushed vehicle.

Eddy carried his son with him down to the basement. He ran over to the water heater and shut it off. He also closed the main gas line to the house. He then carried his son up two flights of stairs, stopping at each room to close the drapes and blinds. When he reached the master bedroom, he saw his other son sitting on the bed amidst the piles of unfolded laundry.

"Daddy," Michael said. Eddy dropped Matthew next to his brother, kissed them both, and turned to find his wife.

His was nervous, almost neurotic but he was trying to put on a good face for Ann.

"Honey, I'm in here." She motioned to him. Through the doorway he could see his wife sipping a Bartles & James with her feet up in the bathtub, her brown hair twirled into a ponytail. She was running her hand over the water spilling out of the faucet.

"You should have enough hot water for a bath but that's it." He removed the almanac from his coat and set it on the counter. "I turned off the gas and the water heater."

She sat up in the tub dripping. "Why?"

"To play it safe. The coroner said it wasn't lightning, Ann. I'm pretty sure the family was murdered."

He went on explaining what Dr. Kemper and Dr. Waverly had shared with him. He could see his wife's fear increasing as he spoke.

"I just saw the news. Dr. Kemper, who I showed the almanac to a couple of hours ago, was killed in an auto accident," he said.

"Our lives are in danger?" she asked.

"Maybe, I think we need to take precautions," Eddy said. "I noticed a black van following me today."

She looked across the room at the drawn blinds. "What are we supposed to do? Live like fugitives with the windows covered and no hot water?"

"I wouldn't use the phone very much either. They've probably got it tapped. I'll call Mark and ask him to get us some protection. We can have a squad car parked outside our house. I'll have a deputy drive you to the health club where you and the boys can shower."

"This is ridiculous. Eddy, give them the almanac."

He sat on the floor next to the tub and whispered. "I've been thinking about that as I drove home. I don't know if handing over the almanac at this point will make much of a difference."

"But that's what they want."

"They want this information kept quiet. How do I know they won't kill me after I give them the almanac? The almanac might be our shield."

Ann poured water over her face, washing away the tears welling up in her brown eyes. "What will we do?"

Eddy rubbed a smudge of mascara off her cheek. "I'll remind them that we're in control here by publishing a story about the weather. I'll say just enough to make the NSA nervous –to get them to back off. That might buy us some breathing room."

"Then what?"

He knew what she was wanted to hear, that he would eventually hand over the almanac. He wasn't ready to do that and he wasn't going to lie to her about it either.

"I don't know what we'll do next. I really don't know."

Joe Simmons had a comfortable hideaway at the bottom end of Louisiana's Mississippi River. This was where the muddy banks widened to a gaping mouth, spewing brown water like a rusty sewer pipe into forests and swamps before it reached the ocean. His houseboat was an easy place to catch birds and he would sometimes hunt right from the deck. The swamp trees also gave him cover from the satellites that he knew were watching from above.

Simmons was licking rolling papers and stacking his homemade smokes in neat piles on the table as he watched his friends, Curtis and Nelles, hacking with his computer. On the table next to him was a half-empty bottle of Jack Daniels - his breakfast of champions.

All the computer equipment inside the ancient boat was state-of-the-art and Simmons had installed a solar-powered generator to run the electricity. His computer had a wireless modem and illegal access to the internet - he'd hacked his way in through a local internet service provider. He'd always felt access to the internet should be free.

Along one entire wall of the boat cabin, he'd installed meters and gauges to measure the weather. He studied the meters now and again when he was sober enough to care what happened in the outside world.

His Cuban friends were Gen-Xers but to Simmons they seemed even younger in the glow of a computer screen.

"¡Carajo! ¡Cojones!" Curtis said, smacking his friend's large potato-shaped head. "You blowing it, man."

Nelles elbowed him sharply in the face. "I got us this far, no?"

"Ahhh, he's blowing it. Right, Joe?"

Simmons tied back his dred-locks with a rubber band and glared at them both, licking the thin paper of another smoke. Nelles and Curtis, weren't really Nelles and Curtis at all. They were illegal immigrants, Cubans that Simmons found making their way to the promised land on a sinking raft.

He'd picked them up, gave them American names, and was surprised to learn that these two had worked for Fidel Castro's propaganda regime. Instead of assembling software code for Communism, they'd spent their free time building a raft. They were much better at software programming.

The two of them dressed like South American guerillas with their green army pants and black boots that tied at mid-shin. He was amazed at their hacking abilities. He'd taught them a few American hacking tricks but the Cubans had surpassed his talents months ago. "You dorks never made it this far into MicroSoft before," Simmons said, reading the screen.

"You got that right," Nelles said in near perfect Hollywood English, as if every word he'd learned was a line from an HBO movie.

"Give me a shot," Curtis said. "I take it from here."

"No way, bro. This is MicroSoft, Bill Gatesville. I'm not handing this hack to you," Nelles said quickly, spitting out the sentence as one long word.

"You suck, man," Curtis said, sitting back with his arms crossed. He had a collection of tattoos that scaled his arms like ivy.

"Bite me," Nelles said.

The young men were perfecting their hacking skills by spreading "internet graffiti" across Websites of multi-national corporations that exploited third world nations. They'd crack their way into the main server of these sites, scale the "firewalls" that every server had to prevent hackers, and they'd reassemble the company's Web pages with their own propaganda.

They didn't work as "hacktivists" out of any sense of righteousness, the three of them did it for the money. Political action groups and small grass roots organizations would filter money to Simmons and he'd spread graffiti on the internet. Sometimes he would get paid a bonus if he "accidentally" downloaded a company's confidential data, such as salary schedules and supplier lists. In the modern information age, Joe Simmons was proud of the fact that he was a corporate pirate that actually lived on a boat.

Simmons glanced at the clock on the screen. He had to watch them or they'd slip up. They were good but sometimes overconfident and sloppy. "If you can break in, do it soon."

"One more password and we're in," Nelles said.

Password or no password, Simmons didn't care. "You've been logged in for nine minutes. Bail out and try later."

"Yo, no fucking way," Nelles said. "This bitch is mine."

"It's been too long," Simmons said. "They'll trace. Log off now."

Nelles clung to the computer like a child at a video game parlor who had already dropped in all his tokens. "But I've made it to the next level."

"They'll trace," Simmons said. Screw these guys, he wasn't getting busted. He walked over to the computer and hit a hotkey that instantly logged him off the Web.

Nelles kicked the desk with his boot. "What the hell?"

"¡Tu eres un soplatubos!" Curtis shouted, calling Simmons an idiot. "You pay us."

"Bets are off, boys," Simmons said.

Curtis forced his greasy face up to Joe's. "You owe us."

"You're taking too many risks to get in," Simmons said. "I'm not heading to jail because you're a screw up."

"That was awesome hacking. They never trace us," Nelles said, shaking the keyboard. "Pay up, Joe."

Simmons tossed them each a bag of weed but Nelles kept his dirty paw out. "Man cannot live on dope alone. ¿The greenbacks, donde estan?"

They were learning fast. For the longest time, Nelles and Curtis weren't money motivated. Suddenly they were changing their terms. They'd seen all the other young punks launching virtual Web companies and making big money on the internet. Why shouldn't they get rich, too?

Simmons walked back to the kitchenette and opened a safe bolted to the counter. Primitive but reliable, he called his safe "Joe's ATM" where he was never charged a withdrawal fee. Inside were rolls of bills. He set a stack on the table for the dogs to sniff. "Why don't you boys go out for recess? Cool off for awhile."

Nelles picked up half of the money. "Fucking Yankee Gringo."

Curtis grabbed his money, followed Nelles to the door and farted, waving his hand by his ass wafting the stench into the air. "Buen provecho."

"You little prick," Simmons said, shoving Curtis out onto the deck.

"It's little, yeah," Nelles said, lighting up a joint. "I seen it."

"Little? It's bigger than yours," Curtis said.

Simmons closed the door and opened the windows in the cabin when he realized he had an e-mail alert from Dr. Kemper flashing on his computer screen. It had been delivered hours before but Nelles and Curtis hadn't bothered to tell him. They were too engrossed with their hacking.

Kemper's letter was an encrypted file. All of his correspondence was sent that way because neither he nor Simmons could be suckered into believing that the internet was free from the roving eye of Big Brother. They knew that every e-mail sent over data networks was copied onto a central server hidden somewhere in Kansas where the NSA used mainframes to read the mail, supposedly in the name of national security.

Simmons launched his homemade software to open and translate the letter that was also written in "Hitakempe" - a language Kemper had invented twenty years before. The language consisted of algebraic equations that spelled geometric shapes that had to be converted with Kemper's homemade alphabet.

Without the software to decode the shapes, it could take Simmons days to translate the letter, which he often found to be an interesting challenge but today he was in no mood. He launched the software and read the letter that Kemper had marked, "Urgent":

Joe,
A farmer here in town found a way into the Weather Program
and he's given the information to a local newspaper reporter.
The farmer is dead. The government is closing in. I'll contact
Sarah Waverly. Come quick and bring the software with you.
Alan

This was amazing news. Simmons sat there for minute feeling the river current rocking his boat. He didn't quite believe it. And what software was Kemper referring to?

He walked back to the cabin door and stepped out into the haze of sunlight where Curtis and Nelles were tanning their brown skin on the deck like two turtles on a log.

"You been reading my e-mail?" he asked.

Nelles took a drag from his joint and held it deep inside his chest, looking over at his friend.

Curtis squinted his cocker spaniel eyes. "¿Por que?"

"Kemper wrote to me about an encryption software," Simmons said.

"He needed a program to crack data," Curtis shrugged. "You were ashore. I sent him some shit you had. Big whoop, no?"

"Pack up, were leaving," Simmons said.

Curtis kept sunning himself. "Right now?"

Simmons reached for a thick rope tied to a dingy just beyond the edge of the boat railing. He began pulling hard, hoisting the wet rope and clumps of mud onto the deck.

"Give me a hand, you lazy asses," he said.

They both staggered up, their smokes pinched between their lips and helped him heave hard on the rope, their tan biceps twitching with each pull. What emerged from the depths of the Mississippi was a large plastic cooler that Simmons hadn't needed in years.

They hauled it onto the boat and he opened the padlocks with a set of keys he'd kept dangling with dog tags chained around his neck. Inside the cooler were six rockets.

Curtis smiled. "Cool."

Simmons opened a thin nylon wallet and removed a small map he'd folded and unfolded one too many times. The creases on the map had frayed and the faded ink was hard to read. He pointed off into the shade of the swamp.

"There's another stash under a fallen log over there," he said. "We'll pick up that load, too."

"Why?" Nelles asked, wiping the mud on his camouflage pants.

"We're bailing out of here," Simmons said. "Pack up. We're in a hurry."

Nelles took a drag and exhaled, speaking through his smoke. "Bailing out? To where?"

"Minnesota," Simmons said, untying the boat from a half-submerged tree.

Curtis looked back at Nelles as if he had no idea where the hell the place was. "¿Minnesota?"

"Up north," Nelles said, pointing over the trees. "Way up north where the stinking river starts."

"¿Por que?" Curtis asked.

Simmons looked out onto the dirty water and up at the clean blueness of the sky. "First we got to stop and meet with Ripper. We need rocket launchers for these babies," he said, cradling a rocket. "Then we head to Minnesota to make the biggest fucking score you could ever imagine."

CHAPTER FOUR

The unusual howling of dogs portends a storm.

LATE TUESDAY EVENING, Mark pulled up to Eddy's driveway in his squad car with a deputy's car close behind. Eddy had the almanac tucked under his windbreaker and he reached out to hug his wife. A neighbor's dog howled at them from the shadows across the street.

"I'll be at the office for a couple of hours," he said. "Get some sleep."

She held him tightly, whispering in his ear. "I'm scared."

"I know. I'll figure this out."

He stepped into the damp night air where Mark was standing on the sidewalk.

"Ken's my best deputy, Ann. He'll keep an eye on things," Mark said. He turned to Eddy adjusting his belt and gun. "Ready when you are, buddy."

They drove to Eddy's office, winding along the farms and gravel roads. Mark followed Eddy's Suburban, keeping his squad car at least five car lengths back. Eddy looked up occasionally at his rearview mirror for a sign of trouble from Mark, while moths and other insects attracted to Eddy's headlights, splattered against his windshield.

Eddy assumed that if somebody were following him they'd come from behind, but up ahead he saw headlights that appeared to be coming toward him in his lane.

He flashed his high-beams and the oncoming vehicle flashed its own, the white light burning Eddy's vision. He picked up the cellular phone on his seat and hit speed dial. "Mark, I need your help!"

Strickland accelerated the van to over seventy miles per hour, right down the center of the flat highway. He had the advantage with his night vision windshield, except for the smear of insects splattered across the glass. Strickland could clearly see Osland's truck illuminated in a wash of green light. He leaned harder on the gas, knowing that Osland would swerve off the road into the ditch and hopefully to his death-or at least he'd be injured bad enough for them to retrieve the almanac.

Manning waved from the seat behind him. "Team Two spotted a squad car trailing Osland."

"Forget the squad car. This will be over in minute," Strickland said, white knuckling the steering wheel, barreling toward Osland's truck. "Why the fuck isn't this guy swerving off the road?"

One hundred yards, fifty yards, thirty yards, and Strickland couldn't hold the line any longer. He swung the van to the right of Osland's truck in a roar of screeching rubber and spitting gravel. As he passed the vehicle, he looked back at his side mirror and realized Osland's truck was parked in the middle of the highway with the back hatch door propped open.

Strickland made a sudden u-turn and twisted the headset closer to his mouth. "Osland's running. I want all teams in the fields on either side of this road! Manning, where is he?"

Manning scanned the monitors. "I'm picking up movement in the field south of the road."

Eddy ran with the almanac across the open field, slipping on clumps of mud with each stride. Up ahead of him was a corn maze the local farmers had carved out of the field during last year's Fall Festival. It was a larger than life maze with corn rows seven feet high. Eddy remembered getting lost in it with his sons. Hearing voices from behind, he ran to the maze for cover.

Sprinting into the dark corridor of foliage, he took a quick left and ran down another straightaway to a right turn that became a dead end. He turned back noticing that the winter and spring winds had left the old corn standing but the walls had warped and bowed as if they were melting. The dry walls reeked of rotting plants.

He ran back down the corridor and took another blind turn sending him deeper into the corn maze. He tried climbing through the walls but they were at least five feet thick and supported by chicken wire. Pausing to catch his breath, Eddy listened for the voices that were getting closer.

"Eddy? It's me, Craig Strickland."

Eddy took two steps back around a turn inside the maze without respond- ing. He was aware of the sloshing sound his feet made in the mud. He could hear Strickland whispering to somebody as he inspected the walls of corn.

"All I want to do is talk, Eddy. Maybe you and I can make a deal."

Eddy heard the snap of a twig and the sound of somebody slipping in the mud in the next aisle over. One of Strickland's men had entered the maze. Eddy moved again down the corridor searching both sides for a turn that didn't hit a dead end but the darkness made it difficult to see the end of each row. He had to run and turn, run and turn, to keep a distance between him and the men following.

"Can you see him, Manning?"

Eddy heard the man in the maze slip again.

"Hell no. It's as dark as a cave in here."

"Don't move," Strickland said to Manning.

A gunshot echoed across the field and Eddy heard a bullet ripping through the corn walls, snapping the dry stalks in half like a weed whipper. Another random gunshot echoed and a bullet buzzed only three feet from Eddy's head. He crouched down low with the almanac in hand.

"What the fuck are you doing?" Manning called out.

"He's in there."

"Goddamn! You nearly shot me," Manning said.

"Come out, Eddy. Don't make me kill you," Strickland said.

They had Eddy trapped and he needed a distraction that would give him an opportunity to break from the maze. He found a book of matches inside his windbreaker pocket and a cigar. He pulled out a match, gave it a strike, and lit the cigar puffing quickly. He then broke it in half and tossed the burning end over the wall to the next aisle. He lit the other half of the cigar and tossed it over as well. He ran down the straightaway and picked up one of the dry corn stalks on the ground. He lit it, and the stalk burst into flames, crackling like a torch and Eddy threw it over the wall to the next aisle as he ran. Behind him he could smell smoke and he could hear Manning shouting.

"Christ! This thing's on fire!" Manning said.

Eddy could hear him stepping on the corn, kicking the walls as if Manning were trying to put out the flames.

"Get out," Strickland shouted.

"I can't find my way," Manning said. "The ground is on fire."

The wind across the open field seemed to stoke the flames and Eddy could see behind him an entire wall of the maze engulfed in and orange glow and thick black smoke. Along the edge of the corridor he could see what looked like an opening, a hole that deer must've made eating their way through the corn during the long winter. He crawled through it and looked out onto the field. A group of agents were running toward the burning maze from the highway.

Eddy ran out of the maze, across the field to a marsh where he jumped into Bluff Creek. He sloshed down the middle of the creek as if he were running down a wet sidewalk in the rain with the almanac in hand. He was backtracking now, peering over the edge of the cattails. Ahead of him, he could see the flashing of red lights. It was Mark's squad car parked on the shoulder of the road.

Mark revved the engine as Eddy climbed out of the creek bed up onto the road.

"I don't believe it," Mark said. "You actually outran those guys."

Mark turned the squad car around as Eddy climbed in the back seat. "Get me to my office as fast as you can!"

When they reached the offices of the *Pioneer Spirit*, Mark walked ahead of Eddy into the dark building. Eddy could see a light on in the back near his office and Mark removed his gun from its holster.

In the shadows of the hallway, a woman rounded the corner in a fast walk. She was carrying something in her arm. Mark raised his gun.

"Freeze!"

She came to a halt, raising her arms slowly, dropping a stack of papers. Eddy realized who she was.

"Hold it! She's my assistant."

"Jesus," Mark said. He lowered the gun and looked at his watch. "She's working awfully late."

"I asked her to meet me here," Eddy said. "I need her for research."

"Mara, this is Mark Barnes," Eddy said.

Mark nodded. "Sorry about that."

"Can I put my arms down now?" she asked.

"Yeah, we thought you were somebody else," Eddy said.

"I'll keep watch outside," Mark said. "You got work to do."

Mara was all business and even though she had noticed the mud on Eddy's shoes and his wet pants legs she said nothing. "Give me one minute and review these ad layouts," she said, picking the sheets off the ground.

Eddy glanced at the ads and gave her a quick approval of the layouts. He was more interested in his own story. "Did you find the information I asked for earlier?"

"You didn't give me much time to research, but I found out a couple of things."

Mara was Eddy's best employee. She was a true research assistant who enjoyed looking up obscure facts. She was fast, efficient, and she could trace down any lead. She was the one who ran behind him at the office managing all the details.

He handed her the layouts and walked down to his office. "These look fine. Print them. What did you find?"

"I located several decent Web sites covering the topic chaos theory. I e-mailed you the links and the background information. I also found a couple of articles about that radical group, Chaotica. What's this all about?"

"I can't get into it, Mara. It's too dangerous," he said walking down the hall to his office. "What about Simmons? Could you track him down?"

"All I can confirm is that he was a student of Dr. Kemper's at the University of Minnesota back in 1965. He was studying math and physics before he went off to Vietnam."

Eddy sat at his desk and turned on his computer. "Nobody has seen or heard from him since?"

"I guess not. He's officially listed as an MIA. The librarian at the university said they have an audio tape of Simmons and Waverly debating chaos theory at a science lecture back in 1964 but that's it."

Eddy remembered that Dr. Waverly had said she and Simmons were students of Dr. Kemper's. "What kind of grades did he get?"

"The university wouldn't release his transcript but they confirmed that he was near the top of his class."

"And he went off to fight a war?"

"He wasn't drafted either. He volunteered."

"What did you find out about Dr. Waverly?"

Mara scrambled through her notes reading off all that she had learned about Sarah Waverly. "Teaches physics and biology at the University of Minnesota and has published a few papers on chaos theory. She was arrested once in college for war protests. Other than that she's pretty clean."

"Can you get me a copy of that audio tape that has Simmons and Waverly debating about chaos theory?"

She smiled and handed him a round aluminum tin. "I went down to the university library this afternoon and picked it up."

Eddy lifted the lid off a musty tin and found a single reel from an old reel to reel tape recorder. He had such a tape player at home somewhere in his basement. "I'll have to listen to this later. Thanks for staying late to help me with this."

"I have to go home and let my dog out." Mara was about to leave his office when she stuck her head back in the door. "Is everything alright, Eddy?"

He looked out the window at Mark's squad car parked under a street lamp. In the reflection of the window Eddy could see the bandage on his forehead, the muddy shoes, and wet pants. "Everything's fine. Believe me, the less you know the better."

He started working on the draft for his article, reading Mara's background information, and typing at his laptop when he received an e-mail. On any given day, Eddy could receive twenty or thirty e-mails from staff members, suppliers, and fellow reporters. He nearly ignored it but he noticed who it was from - Craig Strickland.

He clicked on the e-mail and read the brief message:

While you're trying to remember if you saw the almanac, I took the liberty of helping you look for it. See the attached photos and call me when you're ready to hand the almanac over.

Craig Strickland

Eddy opened the files attached to the e-mail and a photo emerged on his screen. It was a full color picture of his house taken from above. Along the top edge of the picture was today's date and time. The photo had been taken only minutes ago. Eddy could see the deputy's squad car in front of his house. The photo was clear enough that he could read the license plate on the vehicle.

Eddy opened the next file on the screen. It was a photo of him and Dr. Kemper on the Doppler tower. He didn't remember seeing or hearing any aircraft overhead as they had been speaking.

The third photo was of Eddy leaving the arboretum. And the next photo was of him driving the back roads in the rain. This time the shot was tight enough through the windshield he could almost see the almanac on the front seat of his truck.

He opened the last image and it was a picture of him in the office, taken through his window. This picture was different because it was a live video feed. He was watching himself, watching himself. He pushed away from the desk and his image on screen too. He threw the almanac on the floor under his desk and his mirror image on screen did the same. Eddy realized these were satellite images. They were observing his every move from above.

Eddy opened his wallet and found the business card Strickland had given him at the hospital. There was no address information, no name on the card, only a phone number. He dialed the number and after two beeps a man answered.

"Eddy, very impressive move back at the corn maze," Strickland said. "It took all of my men to get Manning out of that tinderbox."

"Call off the dogs," Eddy said.

"Not until you hand over the almanac."

Eddy paced the office, wondering why they hadn't arrested him already. They knew where he was. They could see he had the almanac at this very moment. He figured it must be the fact that he's a reporter. The NSA knew he could spread this information quickly.

"I'm writing a story about the almanac," Eddy said.

"I wouldn't do that if I were you."

"Once I go public with this I'm home free," he said. "You won't be able to touch me."

"Not true. You're a terrorist, Eddy." Strickland asked. "But I'm willing to bargain with you because I trust you."

For a moment, Eddy felt like a terrorist. What he really wanted, information, was something Strickland would never give him.

He decided to test Strickland's resolve. "I want twenty million dollars."

Eddy listened to the long pause on the phone as Strickland pondered the idea.

"Twenty million dollars and you'll hand over the almanac?" Strickland confirmed, without even flinching.

Eddy didn't want the money, he was just stalling, and he realized he'd probably bid too low. "Make that thirty million dollars as soon as possible."

"Slow down. It'll take me a couple of days to set up a Swiss bank account."

"I don't want a Swiss bank account," Eddy said. "Deposit the funds into my account at the State Bank of Chanhassen so I can call in and check the balance."

"I'll see what can be done."

"Tonight I'm writing a story about strange weather that will appear in tomorrow's paper," he said. "Every day that goes by without an increase in my account balance, I'll release more information to the public."

He stopped pacing for a second and pulled the blinds down over the window and the image on his computer screen went dark. He assumed Strickland could no longer see him.

"And no more spying," he said. "If I see a black van or a stranger within ten miles of my family, I'll break the entire story."

He hung up the phone and felt his pulse throbbing in his neck. He had just blackmailed the world's super power. He sat back at his desk and tried printing the images Strickland had e-mailed to him. For some reason his printer wouldn't work. He tried saving them to his hard drive but they simply dissolved into tiny pixels of color on his screen and they were gone.

Eddy looked up the telephone number of Tom DeVaney, an old news hound who used to work with him at UPI who was now a news director at CNN's Atlanta bureau. He called Tom at home knowing it was almost midnight on the East Coast.

"Yeah?" Tom said, in an angry voice.

Eddy tapped his pen on the almanac. "How can you sleep when the world is falling apart?"

"Ah, Jesus, Eddy. What time is it?" he said, muffling the phone.

"What difference does it make? CNN works around the clock and around the world, right?"

Tom laughed. "Don't give me that advertising bullshit. Some of us have to wake up early."

"You're not sleeping tonight, Tom. I've got a big investigative story and I need your help leaking it out slowly."

"Am I dreaming? I thought you weren't covering investigative stories."

"I had a relapse," Eddy said. "What if I told you I had proof that the government controls the global weather system?"

He could hear Tom sitting up in bed, adjusting the phone, possibly grabbing a notepad and pen.

"Go ahead, I'm listening," Tom said.

"I came across a weather almanac that could help me prove Uncle Sam plays games with the weather."

"How would that prove -"

"I don't have a lot of time to explain the details to you now. I've got at least a dozen NSA agents watching me. My phone might be tapped so I'll make this quick. If I send you a story tonight, can you release information first thing in the morning?"

"Sure I'll take a look at what you've got," Tom said.

"If you can forward the information to other news media, I'd sure appreciate," Eddy said.

"Who's our affiliate in your market?" Tom asked.

"My old employer, WMSP TV."

"Yeah, that's it," Tom said. "You should call Alex Andrews and have his team shoot video footage. I'll need visuals of whatever you've got."

At first, Eddy wasn't so sure he wanted Alex Andrews involved in the story but he knew Tom was right. He'd need local help to pull this off. "Thanks, Tom. I'll be in touch."

He hung up the phone and redialed his home number. He was relieved when Ann answered.

"Hello?"

"Just checking in," he said to his wife. "Everything okay?"

He could hear the TV in the background. Ann had tuned into the Weather Channel. He wanted to tell her about the corn maze and the satellites watching her but this wasn't the time or the place.

"We're fine, and you?" she asked.

"Things are improving. I should be home in two hours. I love you."

He noticed a slight pause from his wife, as if she were trying to interpret a hidden meaning to the call. "Get some sleep," he said before hanging up. He took a deep calming breath and started typing.

Eddy knew there was something very intriguing about the weather, it was the one thing that everyone in the world had to deal with. All people are impacted by the weather and everyone has an opinion about the subject. If you asked people, nine times out of ten, they'd boast they could forecast better than the meteorologists in the media.

Eddy decided to tap into everyone's natural frustration with the weather. He wrote an article, titled: *Everyone Talks About the Weather. When Will We Do Something About It?"*

He acknowledged that weather forecasting was eighty percent accurate and improving all the time. He then poked fun at how with all of today's weather forecasting technology you could still go to a picnic during a rainstorm. Why can't they get it right all the time? Eddy suggested in his article that maybe the government officials have more control over the weather than they're admitting. Maybe, he suggested, they're doing something about it and they aren't telling us.

Eddy invited people to write to him with any strange or unusual weather events. He wrote some of this tongue in cheek but he knew the NSA would take it seriously. He then submitted the article to his own newspaper and to Tom DeVaney at CNN.

When Craig Strickland read the Wednesday morning newspaper article written by Eddy Osland, he wasn't overly concerned. The small town newspaper had a circulation of less than fifteen thousand households. Who'd ever heard of the *Pioneer Spirit*? And the article only speculated on the possibility that the government had some control of weather. Osland hadn't actually linked the government to the Jacobsens' murders.

But an early morning phone call came from Strickland's assignment supervisor back in Virginia. Candace McKnight was livid. Her boss, Brent Turks, read Osland's article in *USA Today*. McKnight had read it too, in a section of the *Wall Street Journal*. CNN had published the story on its Website. Within the hour, Strickland found himself sitting in front of the TV in his Chanhassen hotel room, videoconferencing with the head office of the NSA.

He could see McKnight and Turks seated tightly together at the end of a glossy conference room table. Strickland sat on the edge of his bed, drinking Evian from the mini-bar.

"How can this happen?" Turks asked. His movements were short and jerky from the video feed.

"He's a reporter," Strickland rationalized. "He probably made the story available to the newswires."

Turks slammed his fist on the table. The video image vibrated. "I know how he published it. I want to know how he got the almanac?"

"There was handoff between Osland and the farmer," Strickland said.

"What's in this almanac?" Turks asked.

"The farmer downloaded files from the weather database," Strickland said. "We think the almanac might reveal how he gained access."

Candace McKnight eyed him over the rim of her glasses. "By the way, I need your paperwork on that explosion. I hadn't authorized that. And what happened to the meteorologist?"

Strickland sighed. "It'll be in my final report."

"Let me get this straight," Turks said. "You let a reporter get the almanac," he said, restating the obvious.

"We're monitoring him," Strickland said.

"Do you understand why the NSA hired you, Mr. Strickland?" Turks asked.

"Of course."

"Really? I'm having my doubts. Do you think famines actually happen in this day and age? That hurricanes destroy towns and villages? Well, they don't, Mr. Strickland. They're the result of years of mind-boggling, budget-busting computer programming."

"You're preaching to the choir," Strickland said, pointing at the small camera mounted above the TV. "I've worked on the Weather Program since its inception. I don't need a goddamned lecture on how important this is!"

"With all due respect," McKnight said to Turks. "Mr. Strickland was involved in the CIA's Cold War efforts. He's well aware of the importance-"

"I don't give a fuck, Candace," Turks said, continuing. "The Cold War is over. That's why you were reassigned to help us on this case, Mr. Strickland. This Weather Program is our super weapon, our Trojan Horse. It's the best way to keep developing nations under our red, white, and blue thumb. Don't let forty years of government research slip down the drain because some idiot savant in Minnesota breached security. Show us what a big man from the CIA can do!"

Strickland flipped them the finger - off camera.

"He can't walk into Osland's house and take the almanac," McKnight said. "American citizens have rights."

"He says he wants money," Strickland said.

"How much?" McKnight asked.

"Thirty million but he's bluffing."

He watched McKnight turn to her boss. Apparently, thirty million was a little more than she could authorize.

Brent Turks scratched at his chin. "I'll get approval for a funds tranfser. Stall him for a few days."

Strickland nearly fell off the bed onto the cheap hotel carpet. "What? You're not thinking of paying this reporter, are you?"

"Thirty million is a steal, Mr. Strickland," Turks said.

Strickland had traded weapons while at the CIA. He knew how these deals went down. The terrorist always ended up using the guns against you.

"Don't give him the money," Strickland said. "What guarantee do we have that once we pay him he doesn't write about it anyway?"

"What are the other options?" McKnight asked.

"Killing Osland would be the expedient thing to do," Turks said.

McKnight raised her hand, halting the idea. "We've done enough killing. Taking him out now might raise more suspicion."

"Can we forget the theoretical scenarios for a moment and focus on how the real world works?" Strickland asked. "To get the almanac we have to ruin this man. If the CIA were running this manhunt we'd turn his life inside out."

"The NSA has done that before," McKnight said, shrugging the idea off. "Those scenarios require collaboration from too many departments."

Strickland continued. "Smear his name in the press, discredit him. Then take his family away and make a trade. His family is what's most important to him."

McKnight waved her hand in the slow jerky video. "The United States government doesn't kidnap its own citizens."

"Osland is using the media against us. We should use the media against him," Strickland said. "What if something tragic happened to Osland's wife and children and everyone thought he was to blame? We drag his name through the mud, the media creates its own headlines, and we get a warrant to search his house. That would make retrieval a hell of a lot easier."

"I don't think so," McKnight said. "This is not a CIA assignment in Latvia. We're talking about Minnesota."

"I'd rather pay him the money," Turks said.

"I'm telling you he doesn't care about the money," Strickland said. "He told me to deposit the funds into his bank account in Minnesota. He knows we can seize those funds but he also knows that a large sum of money like that in a small town bank requires additional paper work, forms will have to be approved. He's buying himself time."

"Mr. Strickland, I want you to keep a close eye on that reporter," Turks said. "We'll let you know as soon as the money is transferred."

"You're making a big mistake."

McKnight looked up at him shaking her finger. "You'll do this our way or you're out!"

After racing up river all night, trading shifts at the helm, Simmons, Nelles, and Curtis had cruised by the St. Louis Gateway Arch. They were ten miles outside of St. Louis when Simmons pulled over to refill on gas. The filling station was a wooden pier sandwiched by grain barges and tugboats. Simmons glided his houseboat to the pier, tied to a post, and stepped off.

He recognized the skinny man with the tank top shirt sitting on an overturned bucket. He hadn't seen Ripper since he navigated upriver a year ago.

"Look what the river rat dragged in," Ripper said, spitting sunflower seeds into a wet pile on the dock. "What's up?"

Simmons shook his greasy hand. "I need fuel and guns."

He sniffled. "Fuel I got. Guns are harder to come by these days."

Simmons unrolled a wad of bills. "I left my stuff here, man. Hand it over."

"You pawned it and you never came back. I sold that obsolete crap months ago."

"To who?"

"A bunch of military anarchists, you know them weekend warriors, came by," Ripper said, squinting up at him.

"Fuck," Simmons said, looking back at his boat where Curtis had his legs dangling over the bow. Nelles was somewhere below deck. "Where do they hang out? Up river or down?"

"Up river, north of Quad Cities. They got a military camp off near an abandoned grain elevator," he said. "You can't miss it. The grain elevator has an American flag painted on it."

Behind Ripper was a makeshift store with food and drinks. Simmons looked over his supply. "Fill up the boat and I'll take a carton of Marlboros, some beef jerky, and a bottle of Jack Daniels."

Ripper dragged his skinny butt off the bucket and lumbered over to the gas pump. He carried the nozzle and the long snake of a hose to the back of the boat and pumped the gas. When he saw Curtis, he spit. "You're still traveling with Tom Sawyer and Huck Finn, huh?"

"They're traveling with me," Simmons said.

"Aren't you too old to be hanging with drug thugs?"

Simmons inspected the carton of smokes to make sure Ripper hadn't taken a box or two out. "Aren't you too old to be pumping gas?"

"Fuck you, man. It's an honest living."

Simmons picked up Ripper's newspaper and tucked it under his arm. He then walked over to where Ripper was hunched over and shoved a wad of bills into the crack of Ripper's skinny butt. "A grain elevator with an American flag, you said?"

He stood up, counting the money. "Yeah, but instead of stars they painted little white skulls. It's a hoot."

The shades were still drawn shut by mid-morning in the Osland household. Ann was reading Eddy's newspaper column in the *Pioneer Spirit* while the twins played with their trucks on the family room carpet. Eddy was busy threading the reel-to-reel tape recorder that he'd dug up from boxes in the basement.

He was waiting for the fallout from the article. He was curious to find out what his wife thought. "Well?"

She paused for a moment. "If they read this, there'll be no doubt in their mind that you know what's going on," she said in a low, hushed tone.

"They'll read it," he said. "Tom called me early this morning and said the *Wall Street Journal* picked it off the newswire late last night. They ran it in this morning's edition. CNN posted the story on its Website and another fifteen dailies are running it tomorrow."

Ann reached for the phone and dialed it for the second time in thirty minutes. He knew she was checking their bank account.

"We're not rich yet."

Eddy smiled. "No, but you could probably open some of the drapes. I think NSA will give us our privacy. You might even let that deputy go."

She nodded in agreement. "What's on that tape?"

"In the early sixties Joe Simmons and Sarah Waverly were students of Dr. Kempers. They had a heated discussion at a science lecture. I was curious to find out why."

Eddy slipped on pair of headphones and listened to what sounded like a panel discussion where Simmons and Waverly were fielding questions from a audience. It was apparent from where the tape started that this was the second of two reels. The first reel was missing.

"Good afternoon, Ms. Waverly, Mr. Simmons. We've discussed how chaos is really a science that unites all sciences," a woman said. "What are some practical applications of this science in the near future? Thank you."

Waverly spoke first. "I would like to emphasize my belief that the study of chaos is so new, no short-term practical uses could be applied without risking some unexpected side effects. "

"Wait a minute," Simmons said emphatically. "I think we should look at how far we have come. Sir Isaac Newton showed us that math and physics provide a means to study nature, but the pathway has always been very linear. Chaos theory will unlock new doors for all sciences."

"Yes, it will," said Waverly sharply. "We must recognize, however, that we could be opening Pandora's Box by relying on complexity theories in everyday life."

"Relax," Simmons said. "Can't you accept the fact that the study of chaos is really the study of order? In fact, chaos is the very essence of order."

Eddy could hear the tension rising in Waverly's voice. "I understand your point, Mr. Simmons. I'm answering the woman's question, and in my opinion, chaos is more theory than application."

"I can think of a few practical applications," said Simmons. "For example, take a factory that makes cars. At the outset, the factory appears to be a linear system. By calculating the number of employees assembling parts, the amount of time they work, and the number of customer orders, over time you have an accurate model of the throughput of the factory. The factory appears to be a predictable, linear system.

"However, ask any factory manager why she is not meeting production quotas, and she will give you specific reasons that you may not have considered that now alter the equation. Two employees leaving early for PTA meetings, or five of the car orders require special parts to meet customer requirements, and suddenly a very simple linear formula becomes dynamic or chaotic. Chaos theory recognizes that most systems appear linear but are actually more dynamic. The common factory worker deals with complexity theory every day, Ms. Waverly."

"I agree," Waverly said. "Most linear systems are more dynamic than they appear. That's part of fractal reality. But you're saying that by using mathematical formulas you can forecast and predict when somebody will have to go to a PTA meeting." Waverly said. The audience erupted in laughter, and Eddy did too.

"Yes, I am," Simmons said with emphasis.

The audience quieted as Simmons continued. "Let me give you an example we can relate to. The most complex system that we all experience each day is the weather, right? We have meteorologists studying and mapping the weather all over the world. The reason the weather is so difficult to predict is that it is so infinitely complex. Edward Lorenz created a mathematical formulation or what is called an attractor to simulate the complexity of weather systems. He discovered that the attractor, which is the model of a system measured, had to look exactly like the system or you would receive a completely different result."

Simmons paused, and Eddy could hear him walking across the stage. "Could somebody dim the lights, please? Thank you," Simmons said. "The model, or more specifically the attractor that Lorenz created, is based on three equations, three constants, and three time-dependent variables. The weather attractor represents gas at any given time. The conditions of the gas at any given time depend on its condition at a previous time. If the initial conditions are changed by even the smallest amount, the net result of the formula will be different. This is because the changes, no matter how small they start out to be, will propagate themselves recursively until the end result is so different from the original."

Eddy cupped his hands over the headphones listening closely. He could hear Simmons reach for a marker. "Lorenz's attractor looks like two swirling connected circles. If conditions starting here at one end are slightly different at the outset, its path is also different and ends up over here. You'll notice what I have drawn here looks like a butterfly? We call this attractor Lorenz's butterfly."

"Fine. I will indulge you here, Mr. Simmons," Waverly said. "You're saying that by using chaos theory we can more accurately predict the weather. Is that it?"

"Forget about five-day forecasts. In the near future, we will have five-month forecasts. As long as we know the initial conditions, we should be able to predict the outcome elsewhere in the system. We have to recognize that even the smallest change could give us a totally different weather pattern. It's what we call-"

"The Butterfly Effect," Waverly said. "We all know the theory: 'How does a butterfly flapping its wings in South Africa, impact weather elsewhere on the planet?'"

Eddy paused the tape long enough to reach for the almanac on the counter. He paged through it as he listened.

"But this is where complexity theories fall short of day-to-day application," Waverly argued. "Edward Lorenz used his attractor to prove weather systems are too dynamic to forecast accurately more than three or four days. Besides, if chaos is built on a delicate balance of initial conditions, then a complete view of the entire chaotic system would be necessary to measure every particle. In other words, no technology can simultaneously measure all the particles or butterflies in our atmosphere to apply chaos as a weather forecasting tool."

"Oh, but it can," said Simmons.

"Really? What is this new technology?" Waverly asked.

"They're called satellites," Simmons said, pausing briefly for the audience reaction to die down. Eddy knew that back in the early to mid-sixties the United States and Russia were racing to send satellites into space. Simmons's reference to that technology would've been a very hot topic. People were suspicious of satellites back then.

"The satellites could have cameras and lenses to help us look back at our planet. Instead of only tracking cloud formations or hurricane trajectories," Simmons said. "The satellites would look deeper and determine detailed local patterns of wind, temperature, and moisture. Like refocusing their lenses from macro to micro."

A loud hum of excitement filled the auditorium. Waverly spoke loudly to regain control of the room. "Excuse me, please. If satellites could some day carry out such measurements, we run the risk of becoming too dependent on the measuring tool. If your long-range forecasts are dependent on a series of satellites, and if one of those satellites malfunctions, we've got a problem."

"You have to understand that the satellites could act as our lens to monitor the weather, but we would also rely on a device for manipulating the weather," Simmons said. "Russian scientists have been experimenting with weather machines and they're already way ahead of the United States. I would venture to guess that's why the Russians were the first to launch a satellite. They'll use them to support their weather machines."

Sarah laughed. "Weather machines?"

"The well-respected scientist Nikola Tesla used a high-powered radio transmitter to harness the earth's electrical charge. Using what is now known as the Tesla Coil, he was able to create his own lightning in Colorado," Simmons said. "Tesla experimented with ways to supercharge the particles in the atmosphere. Some scientists speculate Tesla accidentally caused the Tunguska explosion in Siberia back in 1908 with a radio tower in New Jersey. His supercharged particles were the equivalent of fifteen megatons of TNT, leveling five hundred acres of forest. If he had had the benefit of satellites, he might have been able to control the weather rather than just play with it."

"I think what you're describing is more folklore than science," Waverly said.

The auditorium burst into discussions and Eddy could hear the panel moderator banging something to regain the audience's attention.

"It's real," Simmons said. "And it's happening right now."

The audio on the tape started cracking and hissing. Eddy could see there was almost no tape left on the feeder reel.

"If the Russians have this kind of technology," Waverly asked. "Are you saying the United States should, too?"

"In the future, weather will be the greatest weapon," Simmons said. "This will be bigger than the atom bomb. History has taught us that we have an obligation to the free world to keep up with technology. Even if we have no intentions of using weather as a weapon, others will."

The tape ran out and spun around the second reel whipping in its circular motion. Eddy removed the headphones.

"Weather as a weapon," he said.

Ann looked back at him from the couch. "Excuse me?"

"I hadn't really thought about *why* the government would do this. Simmons mentions that weather could be a weapon. And if we have the plans for the weapon we could be arrested and tried for treason. That's why Strickland called me a terrorist."

She folded the newspaper with a huff. "Great, and when we're thrown in prison who will take care of our boys?"

"We're not going to prison," Eddy said. "We're going to publicize this. I have a few errands to run this morning. First, I'll go to the WMSP TV and talk to Alex Andrews about covering this story."

"What about the NSA?"

"I told them to back off," Eddy said. "Let's see if they listened."

CHAPTER FIVE

Calm weather in June, sets corn in tune.

THE BLACK VAN was beginning to feel hot and stuffy and Strickland cranked up the air as he sat in the front seat kneading the stress ball in his left hand. They parked near a new office complex a half mile away from WMSP studios. Across the road was a field of mud with small green sprouts soaking up the sun. Strickland was farther away than he felt necessary but he didn't want Osland to see them.

He watched the reporter on the satellite monitors walking into the building with the black notebook under his arm. The cocky bastard wasn't even hiding the almanac anymore.

"There it is," Manning said, pushing his finger on the monitor.

Strickland watched Eddy walk right into the building with the almanac. "And there it goes."

"What should we do?"

"If this were a CIA assignment, I'd walk up and pop him in the lobby," Strickland said.

Manning's face twisted to nausea. "You'd do that in public?"

"I have," Strickland said. "And if Candace McKnight doesn't give me the freedom to run this job as I see fit, I might."

WMSP studios were exactly as Eddy had left them three years before. Even in the late afternoon, the newsroom was teaming with executives running down the halls yelling or shoving their way to the next meeting. Forgetting that he no longer worked at the station, Eddy walked by the main receptionist with a black notebook under his arm and the real almanac under his windbreaker.

The young woman stood immediately and waved a pen. "Excuse me. Are you here to see somebody?"

Eddy didn't recognize her. Her securityguard attitude bothered him. He forced a smile. "I used to work here. Who are you?"

"Kathleen. I'm the day receptionist. And you are?" she asked, searching his face for an answer.

It was one thing for a perfect stranger not to recognize Eddy, but here was a WMSP employee who didn't have a clue as to who he was.

Fame wears off quickly, he thought. "Eddy Osland. I'm here to see Alex Andrews. Don't bother yourself. I know where his office is."

Passing through the newsroom, he finally caught the attention of some of the core people at the TV station. Rick, the evening news director, was on the phone and waved. Jason Hurley, who had been a college intern the last time Eddy saw him, was typing on a keyboard.

"Hey, Eddy," Jason said, reaching out his hand.

"I need to see Alex."

"He's around here somewhere," Jason said. "Follow me."

Jason led him into a large office with a glass conference room table at one end and a large bookshelf with trophies on the far wall. At the other end of the room was a large cherrywood desk.

Eddy could smell Alex's stale cologne hanging in the air. "This is his office?"

"He's producing now. Global Media WorldWide gave him a big bump in salary and some cash incentives to boost ratings. I guess the new office goes with the territory," Jason said.

Eddy examined the room. New carpet, a big desk, coffeepot. Outside the door, all the other staffers had cubicles. "If he got a big promotion, why do I see him on the air covering stories?"

"Because he's Alex Andrews. You know, the big ego won't let go," Jason said, pushing his glasses up on his nose.

"How about you, Jason? You hung around long enough they finally decided to pay you?"

"They hired me not long after you left," Jason said, cracking his knuckles. "They made management changes. I'm working for Alex."

"Oh, I'm sorry to hear that," Eddy said, moving across the room to read the media awards on the bookshelf.

Alex entered with a big open hand and a gaping smile. "Ozzie, what an unexpected surprise."

Eddy closed his door. "I have a story for you."

"Really? An exclusive?" Alex asked.

"It's too big a story to give you an exclusive," Eddy said. "You'll have to work with Tom DeVaney at CNN."

"Alright, I know Tom. What kind of story?" Alex asked.

"At the farm on Monday I picked up some evidence that the government doesn't want the public to see," Eddy said.

"Evidence of what?" Jason asked.

Alex shot him a stare. "Thanks, Jason. I think I can handle it from here."

"Evidence of murder and proof that the government is controlling the global weather system," Eddy said.

Alex blinked at the thought of it. "I read your article in the paper this morning. Is that what this is about?"

"It's a huge conspiracy, Alex. One that could make you and me famous," he said, playing to Alex's narcissism.

He set the blank notebook on Alex's desk and removed the almanac from his windbreaker. He let Alex page through it as Jason read over his shoulder. He spent several minutes explaining as many of the details as he could piece together.

"I think we should work together to cover the story," Eddy said. "I need access to the resources of a large investigative team. I want to hit the airwaves with the full story soon. I need local support."

Alex handed him back the almanac. "It's very cool, Ozzie. But I don't think the station management will go for it."

Eddy couldn't believe the words that had dripped out of Alex's mouth. "What do mean the station won't go for it? CNN is interested in it."

"The evidence is too anecdotal," he said. "Has Tom DeVaney seen this almanac? You've got a handwritten diary here from a farmer who probably watched the Weather Channel."

"He's more accurate than the Weather Channel," Eddy said.

"And you're linking all these deaths together," Alex said. "Again, it's hearsay. When it comes to investigative stories our legal department has really cracked down."

"Alex is right," Jason said. "Upper management is afraid of getting sued or alienating advertisers."

Eddy knew what they were saying. There were many legal hoops to jump through to cover investigative stories. And each hoop was narrower than the next.

"Do you believe me, Alex?" Eddy asked.

He hesitated for second. It was subtle, but Eddy noticed it.

"Sure, I can see how you came up with this theory."

"You don't believe me."

"More evidence would give you a stronger case here," Alex said.

"If I can show you how the farmer downloaded the data? If you saw it for yourself would that convince you?" Eddy asked.

"Sure, if we can videotape how he did it, then I think we have a story here," Alex said.

Eddy stuffed the almanac inside his jacket. "I'll call you when I'm ready. And if anything should happen to me in the meantime, call Tom DeVaney."

He left the office and Alex called to him, waving the empty notebook Eddy had intentionally left on his desk. "What am I supposed to do with this?"

"Hold onto it and watch what happens," Eddy said.

He walked out of the building into the warm early afternoon sun, the real almanac tucked inside his windbreaker. He raised his empty hands up in the air where he assumed a satellite was taking his picture.

The stress ball flew across the van and smacked one of the monitors above Manning's head. On several screens were shots of Eddy walking back to his truck carrying nothing.

Strickland pulled the headset from his neck up onto his ears. Fuck the damn money, he thought to himself. "Osland has made a hand-off. I want all teams at the WMSP studio now."

He put the van in gear and made a u-turn. Manning fell out of his seat and struggled to climb back in as they drove.

"See what happens when we sit on our asses?" he said to Manning. "You NSA agents don't know how to get the job done. That fucking Candace McKnight."

When they reached the TV station, two of the other four vans arrived at the same time. The agents piled out of the darkness of their vehicles and ran into the station with Strickland leading the pack.

He flashed the receptionist ID and looked down at the sign-in sheet. "Who was Edward Osland here to see?"

"Alex Andrews but you can't go back there."

Strickland ran down the hall with the other seven agents right behind him. He searched for nameplates on office doors and cubicles, he quickly analyzed confused faces. The agents split up, and filtered through the office, all of them calling Alex's name.

Strickland saw a man standing in a doorway with a black notebook in hand. He raised his weapon and pointed it at the man as a shriek of terror echoed through the office. Everyone but the agents and the man in the doorway dropped to the floor.

"I'm Alex Andrews," he said. "What's going on?"

Strickland walked up to him. "National Security Agency. Drop the notebook, Mr. Andrews. Hands above your head."

"Why?"

"Drop the notebook!"

Strickland could see Alex's heart banging in his chest so that his tie throbbed up and down. Alex let the notebook fall to the floor and raised his hands above his head. Strickland walked over and picked it up. He raised the notebook up where all the other agents could see it.

He thumbed through the empty pages with a sick feeling in the pit of his stomach. On the inside front cover was a note from Osland.

> *"Are you following me? That cost you another ten million dollars."*
>
>   *Eddy Osland*

"Shit!" Strickland threw the notebook at Manning's feet.

"Would somebody tell me what's going on?" Alex said.

"Nothing, we apologize for the disturbance," Strickland said, walking back to the reception desk. Behind him he could hear the hustle of confusion from the office workers. A videographer tried to capture the moment on tape and two of Strickland's agents wrestled the camera to the floor.

Strickland stepped outside, looking around the parking lot. An agent from one of the teams that hadn't arrived yet crackled in his headset. "We see Osland heading for the highway."

"Let him go."

"I'm sorry," the agent said. "Did you say-"

"Give him the breathing room that he wants," Strickland said. "I want you out at Osland's house to search for the almanac."

"It's the middle of the day, sir. The family is home."

Strickland was tired of waiting and watching Osland. And he knew asking McKnight to scrounge up another ten million dollars would only delay things further. It was time to do things the old fashioned way. "If we can't find the almanac, we're taking his wife and kids!"

Eddy drove his old Suburban down a gravel road with bitter smell of manure wafting off the prairie into his side window. The broken gas gauge bobbed back and forth, like a metronome that had no sense of rhythm. He kept looking back but he didn't see anyone following him. He wasn't sure how Strickland would've reacted to the fake almanac but it seemed to put some distance between him and the NSA.

Turning sharply to the right, he drove across a deep field of prairie grass. The afternoon sun burned through the haze like a magnifying glass burning through paper. He flipped through the almanac with one hand and steered with the other. Today was exactly as Mick had forecast.

Arnie Blake, the Midwest Farms sales representative that Eddy had met at the autopsy, was waiting outside his pickup truck at the edge of the field.

He spit chew and smiled at Eddy. "You're late."

"Running from the government is hard work. I just make it look easy," he said, stepping out of his truck. "Do you have the satellite sensor?"

"Yeah, this is the same model Mick used." Blake lifted a small carton no larger than a shoebox out of the back of his flatbed.

Eddy looked around the field to make sure nobody was nearby. "Don't look up."

"Huh?"

"They could be watching us from a satellite," Eddy said.

Arnie Blake's eye peered upward, wrinkling his bald head. "I'll be damned."

"I don't have a lot of time. How does this thing work?"

"It's easy. It comes with an instruction booklet and software. Plug the sensor into the back of your computer's modem port and you're ready to go."

Eddy set the box inside his truck next to the almanac.

Blake leaned in and whispered, as if he thought they could hear him from way up there. "What's this all about anyway?"

"If I tell you, they'll kill you." Eddy climbed into his truck and slammed the door. He started the engine and leaned his elbow out the side window. "Still want to know?"

"No, not really." Blake spit onto the grass. "I'll read about it in the newspaper."

Eddy backed up and stepped on the gas. "Let's hope so."

Eddy had almost everything he needed to prove that the government controlled the weather. He had the almanac with Mick's description of how to rewire the satellite sensor. He had the satellite sensor as well. The only thing missing from the equation was the critical software that could translate the encrypted data.

Joe Simmons had the software and Eddy had no way of reaching him. He used his cellular phone to make a quick call to Dr. Sarah Waverly at the Minnesota Landscape Arboretum. She at least knew of Simmons. He figured if she wouldn't get involved, she could at least make contact for him.

"Landscape Arboretum," a receptionist said.

Eddy cradled the phone against his shoulder as he drove. "Dr. Sarah Waverly, please."

"She's not in."

"Do you expect her soon?"

"Who is this, please?"

He detected a suspicious tone in this woman's voice. "I'm a friend."

"We're not sure where she is. She left work suddenly yesterday and she hasn't shown up this morning."

Eddy knew that wasn't good news. Waverly had told him he was tainted, the NSA had photos of him entering her building, and now she was gone. He hung up the phone and tossed it across his seat. How could he translate the encrypted data?

He nearly passed the Chanhassen Kinko's Copies when he slowed and turned into the parking lot. He hadn't planned to make a copy of the almanac. For some reason, it seemed like the right thing to do. If this was the only thing keeping him alive, why not make another copy?

He looked around, entering the store cautiously. The store was bright and clean, and the smell of copier toner permeated the air. No agents.

"Can I help you?" a teenager with four gold hoops in his left ear asked.

He hardly seemed like a model employee, Eddy thought, handing him the almanac. "I need one copy of this," he said, noticing the teenager's name tag read "Elvis".

"You want it spiral bound like this?" Elvis asked.

"Yes."

"It'll be a couple of hours."

"I can't wait that long," Eddy said, removing his wallet. "How much will it cost to have you copy it right now while I wait?"

Elvis searched the store, as if this might get him in trouble with the manager. "How about an extra ten dollars?"

"Good, I'll wait." Eddy picked up a brochure and held it in front of his face, pretending to be reading, but he was really watching the parking lot. The brochure caught his eye because it was a listing of all the Kinko's in the country.

"How many stores do you have, Elvis?"

"Nineteen Kinko's in Minnesota."

"How many nationwide?" Eddy asked.

"About eight hundred, five stores on the Hawaiian islands."

Eddy turned a page of the brochure. Maui might be a good place to hide his backup copy. It would be foolish to keep it with him. "How hard would it be to make a copy of that to be delivered to your store in Maui?"

Elvis opened the almanac making a visual page count. "Be easy. I scan these pages and send the file by modem. It's also cheaper than shipping."

Entering Osland's house was surprisingly easy because the sheriff's deputy wasn't there. Strickland, along with agents Lisa Wentz and Carl Bentsen, parked up the street waiting for Roy Manning to decipher the code to the Osland's electronic garage door opener. When Manning found the code, Strickland drove up the driveway and right into the garage next to the minivan. "Close the door."

Manning pressed a button on his hand-held receiver and the garage door went down. Before opening the van door, Strickland reminded them of their roles.

"I'll deal with Mrs. Osland if necessary. Agents Bentsen and Manning will search for the almanac on the main floor. Agent Wentz, you search the upper level. If we don't find it, we take wife and kids."

He yanked open the van door just as Ann Osland opened the door from the house to see who was in her garage. Agent Bentsen reached her door first and she slammed it on his arm. He pushed hard with his shoulder and Ann screamed, thrusting the door back, attempting to lock it.

Manning and Bentsen gave a count of three and kicked the door in with a hollow thud as the knob wedged into the wall behind it.

Strickland followed the three agents into the kitchen, all of them wielding their guns. Ann backed away from them reaching for a carving knife in the butcher block.

"Mrs. Osland, we're here for the almanac," Strickland said. "No more games now. Where is it?"

"You can't barge into my home like this," she said. She was breathing hard, almost hyperventilating with fear. "This is against the law."

"You're a terrorist, a threat to national security," Strickland said. "You don't have as many rights as you think. Where's the almanac?"

He moved toward her and she held her ground. "It's not here."

Strickland didn't believe her. "Search the house."

Manning and Bentsen started opening drawers and cabinets in the kitchen first and then the made their way across the house to the family room and living room. They sifted through magazines and books. They tossed the cushions off the couch. Strickland could see she was upset by how they were tearing apart her home.

"I'm telling you the almanac isn't here," she said.

"Agent Wentz and Bentsen, search the upstairs," Strickland said. His gun was still pointed at Ann.

"No! My children are up there," she said.

Strickland ignored her. "Manning, go down to the basement."

Eddy watched Elvis scan the final pages of the almanac. He was nervous. This was taking longer than he'd expected.

"How's that coming?" he asked.

"Finished. I'm sending the file to the store now," Elvis said, typing on a computer. "Business or pleasure?"

Eddy checked his watch and searched the parking lot for suspicious activity. "Pardon me?"

"Going to Maui for business or pleasure?"

He thought about that for a good long moment. Was he really planning a trip to Maui? Why would he need a backup copy of the almanac if he planned to publicize this story? He wasn't really sure.

Manning ran back upstairs to the kitchen. "No almanac in the basement."

Strickland was irritated. He was getting more anxious by the minute. "Anything upstairs?" he called out to Wentz and Bentsen.

He could hear the banging of drawers as Bentsen yelled back. "Nothing so far."

Strickland moved closer to Ann. "I told your husband this would be a lot easier for everyone if he'd cooperate."

Ann swung the large blade hard enough that Strickland felt the breeze it made in the air.

"Stay back," she said.

"You're coming with us, Ann. Give me the knife."

She pointed it directly at him and then she pointed it at Manning.

"It's four of us and one of you," Strickland said. "Give me the knife."

She backed away but Strickland knew she wouldn't leave the house without her children. "Bring down the boys," he said to the agents upstairs.

"Leave my sons alone!"

Agents Wentz and Bentsen came running downstairs to the kitchen with a sleepy boy in each of their arms.

The boy Bentsen held lifted his head. "Momma?"

Ann trembled. "Hi, honey. It's alright."

"Put them in the van," Strickland said.

"No!" Ann screamed.

"Where's the almanac?" Stricklad asked for a final time.

Ann broke down, sobbing through her words. "I don't have it. I'm telling you the truth."

"Then you're coming with us," Strickland said, cocking his gun.

She didn't resist him. She gave in and set the knife on the table in a move that Strickland assumed was intended to protect her children. Manning pushed her out the door to the dark garage and into the van. Bentsen and Wentz followed with the twins. Strickland looked around the destroyed house one last time but couldn't find the almanac.

"Ready to plant trace evidence," Benstsen said, returning with a large toolbox.

Strickland strapped his gun back in its holster. "Draw blood samples from all of them. Plant them in the master bath."

CHAPTER SIX

Birds stop singing and trees become dark
before a storm.

THE FIRST THING Eddy noticed as he arrived home was that the deputy's car wasn't out front. It was his idea to go without the protection. He told Ann that after writing the article they wouldn't need the deputy around the clock, but he had a bad feeling about it now. He drove into the open garage, parked the truck, and went inside with the almanac and the satellite sensor.

He immediately sensed something was wrong. The house was silent. The window above the kitchen sink was open but no sound came from the outside either. No barking dogs, no birds chirping.

"Ann?"

No answer. The kitchen cupboards and drawers were open. He noticed across the room couch cushions were on the floor and magazines were strewn about. The twins could make a mess but they weren't capable of this.

"Ann?!"

Eddy ran up to the bedrooms. The mattress in their room had been pulled from the bed. All the drawers were half opened. In the twins' room their small clothes had been pulled from the rack in the closet, and thrown on the floor.

Eddy ran to the phone and dialed frantically.

"Sheriff's department," the woman said.

"Mark Barnes, please."

"He's on patrol."

"This is his friend, Eddy Osland. It's an emergency."

Eddy ran downstairs as he waited to be patched through to Mark. He took the almanac on the counter and tried to find a place to hide it. He was afraid they'd come back here again. In one of the open drawers he saw a box of Ziploc freezer bags and he decided that's where he'd keep the almanac and the satellite sensor - in the freezer.

"Eddy?" Mark said into the phone. "What's wrong?"

"They were here in my house. They've taken Ann and the boys," he said as he shoved the almanac and satellite sensor box to the back of the freezer.

"Sit tight, I'll be right there," Mark said.

Eddy hung up the phone and stared at the mess. A wave of guilt washed over him as he stood in that room. What kind of man jeopardizes his family's safety? Why did he think he could get away with this? He was dealing with professionals here. People who were paid by the government to lie and steal and to think like chess champions - always five or six moves ahead.

What was Strickland planning to do next? Eddy opened his wallet, found Strickland's business card, and dialed the number. It beeped like it had the first time he'd called but this time there was no answer, no voice-mail, just a continuous beep.

Sheriff Mark Barnes and agent Dick Jeffries from the FBI followed Eddy around the dining room, through the kitchen, into the family room stepping over magazines, toys, and other debris. Jeffries carefully instructed them not to touch anything as they surveyed the house.

"Doesn't add up," Jeffries said. "There's no ransom note."

Eddy checked his caller ID. No calls. "Maybe they'll contact me later."

"And nothing's been stolen from your home?" Jeffries confirmed.

"Except my wife and two sons," Eddy said.

Jeffries rubbed his wrinkled brow. "Looks like we might have a forced entry through the garage door."

"What do you mean we might?" Eddy said. "The doorknob knocked a hole in the wall."

Agent Jeffries kept circling the room with his hands clasped behind his back, as if he were resisting the temptation to pick things up to inspect them.

"Do you know who might've done this?" Jeffries asked.

Eddy looked to Mark. He was surprised his friend hadn't told Jeffries already. Eddy realized it was because it sounded so ludicrous. "I think people from the government."

"The government," Jeffries said, echoing his words.

"Yeah, it's a long story," Eddy said. "I came across a piece of information that's highly classified."

"We think the NSA took Eddy's wife and kids so they could get it back," Mark said.

"Get what back?" Jeffries asked.

"A weather almanac," Eddy said, knowing that to an outsider all of this might sound a little crazy.

"And this almanac is classified information because why?" Jeffries asked.

Eddy noticed the cool skepticism on the FBI agent's face. He realized this is how the rest of the world might react when they hear about the almanac.

"It doesn't matter right now," Eddy said. "Let's focus on getting my family back."

Mark walked over to Jeffries. "You can help us, can't you?"

"I'll get a team out here to see what we can find," he said. "They aren't missing persons until they've been gone twenty-four hours. In the meantime, I'd like you, Mr. Osland, to come down to our office to fill out a report and to answer a few more questions."

North of Quad cities, the Mississippi River had a nasty stink about it, sort of a blend between sewage and diesel fuel. The darkness of the night made it difficult for Simmons to navigate around the inevitable logs floating down river or the sandbars that sat just below the surface like the round backs of submerged hippos.

Nelles and Curtis sat on the bow with searchlights scanning the water's surface, occasionally raising their beams toward the shore's edge.

"Sandbar, a la izquierda," Nelles said.

"Habla en ingles," Simmons said. "Is it to the left or right?"

Nelles waved his flashlight. Simmons accelerated and steered to the right, his old rebuilt engine roaring to life like an angry bull. Pushing, pushing, pushing upriver against the wake.

Ordinarily he'd pull over and camp. He didn't like the river at night. It was an entirely different place, like Vietnam after dark with its thick brush, its shadows, and unusual sounds. But he had guns to collect and he was feeling rather anxious about it.

Curtis sang a verse from the National Anthem that echoed up and down the river. "Oh . . . oh say can you seeeeeeee, by the dawn's early light . . .

At the end of his white beam of light was an American flag painted on the side of a dilapidated grain elevator that stood three stories above the river's edge.

Simmons slowed the boat to a quieter speed, enough to keep them from drifting down river. The flag was exactly as Ripper had described it; red and white stripes, a blue box, with fifty white skulls instead of stars. Simmons pondered whether these people were pro or anti-American? He thought about what his veteran friends would think of a flag like that. They'd kick the ass of the traitor that had painted it. Simmons reached over for his sawed-off shotgun. Maybe he'd have to kick some ass, too.

"What now?" Nelles called back.

"Shhh. ¡Subuso!" is all he said. "Lights down."

The boat hovered there in the middle of the river. The water slapping along the edge gave Simmons the sensation that they were moving but he knew better. A moon above them cast a pale glow on the water and on the grain elevator.

He listened and smelled the air for signs of life from the camp behind the elevator. He'd learned from his days behind enemy lines to sit and keep his mouth shut. Don't run unless you absolutely need to. Don't step without studying the ground first or you might end up paying for a shoe you'll never need. He smelled a campfire and the aroma of bratwurst billowing in the air. Somebody was eating dinner.

Nelles climbed the short ladder to the boat's helm. "Looks like the place, no?"

"Does to me," Simmons said, eyeing the twisted trees along the sandy edge of the river.

"Give me money. Curtis and I go ashore and buy what they got."

"I'm not buying back what's already mine."

"Ah."

"Let's see what these military boys are made of," Simmons said. "Load up the bottle rockets."

There was a twinkle of sinister moonlight in Nelles's eyes. "Si, mi Capitan." He saluted with the wrong hand and jumped down the short flight of stairs, to the back of the boat.

Bottle rockets, or "los cohetes de botella" as Nelles and Curtis called them, was a term Simmons used for the handmade cluster bombs he crafted out of chunks of metal and rusty nails held together by plaster. When the bombs hit their target, they would shatter like glass, sending the shrapnel in a thousand directions. The bombs wouldn't kill you, but they'd mess you up pretty bad. He'd tried them out a couple of times on drug dealers in the Gulf and was always impressed with how quickly they got people's attention.

"Can I run el Barón?" Curtis asked.

Simmons nodded. The kid ran into the bowels of the boat and returned with an old Gatling gun, the kind of machine gun that you had to feed a belt of ammunition. They called it the Baron because it resembled the gun the Red Baron used on the front of his airplane, but this one sat mounted on the front of their boat.

Simmons lifted a pair of binoculars to his eyes and watched for movement near the grain elevator. "Ready when you are, Nelles."

Eddy had spent the entire afternoon and evening at the FBI reviewing the events that led up the disappearance of Ann and the boys. He'd explained everything so many times to Jeffries and his staff, that he was finally confusing himself.

They kept picking at details that he felt weren't important. Jeffries wanted to know how often he and his wife argued. Had he ever hit her before? How did he get the cut on his forehead? Nobody at the Bureau cared about Mick Jacobsen's death, the explosion, or Kemper's car accident. They kept focusing their investigation on Eddy as if he had faked the kidnapping.

When Carl Grady entered with Mark Barnes, Eddy knew things had taken a turn for the worse. Carl was Eddy's attorney, a man who had successfully defended him in libel cases and other legal problems that came with investigative reporting. His friend Mark had a worried look on his face.

"Carl, what are you-"

"I called him," Mark answered.

Carl closed the door and set his briefcase on the table. He unbuttoned his vest so his soft belly could rest comfortably in his lap. "I wish you would've called me earlier, Eddy. Have they read you your rights?"

"Yeah, so?"

Carl sighed. "You're a suspect, Eddy. You're officially under arrest."

"Under arrest? For what?"

"The murder of Ann and the boys," Mark said.

"That's crazy!" Eddy pushed his chair back away from the table.

"Of course it's crazy," Mark said. "That's why I called Carl."

"Somebody's pulling strings here," Eddy said, thinking of Strickland and the power that went with this job. "The NSA is orchestrating this."

"Be careful what you say and how you act," Carl warned.

Eddy took several deep breaths to calm himself down. "Rattle some cages. Don't let them do this to me, Carl."

"I'm here to defend you, Eddy. I'll do everything I can to bring this to an end."

It occurred to Eddy how unbelievable this was. "They can't arrest me if they have no bodies."

"No, but they found traces of blood in the back of the van," Carl said.

Mark took off his sheriff's hat and fussed with the brim. "It matches Ann's blood type."

"Maybe she cut her hand a long time ago removing groceries from the van," Eddy said. "That doesn't prove I'm a murderer."

"The FBI has a search warrant and is combing your house," Carl said. "They've found bloodstains in the bathtub. It's obvious somebody tried to clean it up, but it's visible with infrared light."

"Why would I murder my own family?"

"Eddy, you have life insurance on your wife and both of your children," Carl said.

"So?"

"And you have debts, a large mortgage, a loan on the minivan, a struggling newspaper business," Carl said.

"But the NSA obviously knows that," Eddy said. "They're setting me up."

"Relax. When it comes to murder, family members are always considered suspects," Carl said. "This will blow over."

"This isn't about murder," Eddy said, before stopping himself. They'd found blood in the van and in the bathtub. His chest tightened, his head pounded. "My god, Mark," he said. "They wouldn't have killed my family would they?"

"I don't know, Eddy," Mark said. "I think we should operate on the assumption that they're alive.

"They found blood in the bathtub," Eddy said. "And they'd cleaned it up."

"Maybe Ann resisted them," Mark said. "But they wouldn't kill her."

"I've never seen anything like this before," Carl said, attempting to bring the conversation back to the legalities of all of this. "They're rushing to justice here. Somebody's railroading this thing through."

"It's the NSA," Eddy said. "I know who did it."

"You're innocent until proven guilty," Carl said. "As a defendant we don't need to prove who did it."

"I need to," he said. He stood up and walked to the door, but it was locked. "The government's framing me."

Carl raised his hand, looking around the room. "I wouldn't recommend using that as our defense. Do you know how many convicted criminals claim that the government framed them?"

"I know it sounds outlandish," Eddy said. "But it's true."

"I've scheduled a bail hearing first thing tomorrow morning," Carl said. "Judge Henderson could be tough on us. She doesn't like domestic disputes."

Eddy felt dizzy with grief. He grabbed the chair to steady himself.

"You'll be spending the night in jail," Mark said.

The first cluster bomb that Nelles had launched hit a tree and sprayed shrapnel onto the river below. Simmons watched him aim the rocket launcher higher and the next three bottle rockets arched over the tree line and shattered against something Simmons couldn't see - trees or rocks.

Curtis sat calmly behind the Gatling gun scanning the beach back and forth. "Lucy, I'm home," he shouted in his Cuban accent that sounded a hell of a lot like the real Ricky Ricardo.

Two men ran out of the brush and nestled in along the sand dunes. Simmons could see they had sophisticated gear, too. Both men had helmets with night vision visors and their bodies wrapped in bulletproof jackets. The guns were some variety of AK-47. Fuck, Simmons thought. This won't be a walk in the park.

He yelled to them. "Good evening. We're looking for weapons and ammunition we may've misplaced along the river. Have you found anything like that?"

The reply came in the form of a shower of bullets into the side of Simmons's boat. Curtis crouched down behind his big gun casually until the shower of bullets stopped, as if the men were only spraying him with water.

"I'll take that as a yes," Simmons said. He shoved the boat's throttle down to the floor and the vessel lunged up out of the water at an angle high enough that the bullets from the machine guns hit nothing but the underbelly.

As they neared the shoreline, Simmons slowed enough for the bow of the boat to lower. Curtis opened fire with the Baron in a loud rhythm of shells bouncing around him on the deck. He sprayed up and down the beach like a weekend gardener tending his daisies, back and forth, back and forth.

Nelles aimed the rocket launcher at a horizontal angle and let rip with a bottle rocket that hit the grain elevator and sent nails and metal into the air above the men's heads like hail.

Except for the rumbling of the boat motor, there was a brief moment of silence. The kind of "reload moment" Simmons hadn't thought about since Vietnam. Both sides were checking to see who had been hit, hurt, or killed.

"Fuck," one of the wounded men said.

Simmons lifted his binoculars and searched the brush. "They're moving toward the grain elevator."

Simmons turned the boat around and drifted down river following the movement in the brush. A flash of gunfire came at them again from behind a sand dune.

"I see," Nelles shouted. "One dude's at the door."

Nelles launched another bottle rocket at the building, this time it nearly hit the door where the man was trying to get inside the elevator. He fell in the doorway and covered his face with a shrieking cry. Simmons had heard that sound many times before. Men who were hit by landmines or grenades would often scream more at the surprise of being hit than they would about the pain.

"I dropped him," Nelles said.

The man in the doorway sat up and began shooting rounds at the boat as his partner ran across the open beach to the doorway with him.

"Fire, Curtis," Simmons said.

Curtis finished reloading and cranked the Baron in the direction of the running man. Simmons could see him sighting the moving target, getting the Baron just ahead of the runner before he let loose with a storm of bullets that flew at the runner like a swarm of angry bees. The man collapsed in mid-stride and tumbled across the sand.

"Levántate," Curtis shouted, at the man to get up. "¡Vamos! Come on!"

"You iced him," Simmons said, looking through the binoculars. The man on the beach sprawled out with his face planted in the sand. The only movement Simmons could see was blood and intestines oozing from his stomach. The chest didn't rise and fall with the kind of heavy breathing that accompanies a trauma like that. The man on beach looked young, about twenty-five years old, but he was much older than the boys Simmons had seen die that way in the jungle.

"Watch him, Curtis," Nelles said, pointing to the shrapnel victim in the doorway.

He was standing, unlocking the door. Curtis fired at him but he managed to get inside the grain elevator before the bullets hit the door.

"That's where they keep the guns," Simmons said, steering the boat around a sandbar. "Let's go ashore."

Simmons steered them onto the beach. Nelles jumped into the cold waist-deep water first with Curtis and Simmons following him. They all carried their sawed-off shotguns above their heads. The sawed-offs were no match for the firepower the man had inside the elevator, but that's why they were here.

Together they ran up the beach watching for the gunman. Curtis walked over to the dead man to inspect his handiwork. He checked the AK-47 but the gun was out of ammo and he left it behind. "Vaya con Dios," he said in almost a whisper.

Simmons approached the doorway carefully with his gun out in front of him. The closed door was pock marked with bullets and the padlock that the man had been struggling with was in the sand. He was there. Simmons knew the gunman was standing or crouching on the other side of the door with god knows what kind of weapon.

He motioned to his friends with his fingers, one, two, three. Together they each shot their sawed-offs and the door flew right off its rusty hinges into the building. Simmons was right, the man was there but the door knocked him off balance and his return fire only coated the inside of the building. He scrambled to his feet and ran deeper into the shadows of the elevator like a cockroach heading for the safety of the cupboard after somebody turned on the kitchen light.

They walked into the building, Simmons leading the way. The place was dark except for moonlight streaming in through the patchy holes in the cement walls, illuminating the remnant grain dust in the air.

There were wooden crates in the center of the room and Simmons walked over to see if they'd found what they were looking for. He pried one open and inside there were guns, but not the ones he'd pawned on Ripper. These anti-aircraft missile launchers looked new, straight from the Chinese factory. Nobody buys American anymore, Simmons thought.

Curtis opened another crate and found rounds of ammunition.

Nelles kicked open a box of food rations. "Tienen un coco con el año dos mil," he whispered to Curtis.

"Translation?" Simmons said.

Curtis sniffled. "Y2kers."

They all heard the creaking sound of footsteps on the next level up. Simmons looked up to a large hole in the center of the ceiling, just above the guns and ammunition. They were vulnerable here because the man could easily shoot down at them. Simmons backed away from the hole, surveying the building trying to figure out how to get up there.

Behind Simmons, Curtis and Nelles were whispering in Spanish. They would do that occasionally, they'd jump between English and Spanish without realizing it. Simmons knew that they usually did it when they were nervous, when their Cuban brains had no time to translate.

He turned to look at them. They were staring up through a hole in the ceiling.

"What?" Simmons said.

Curtis whispered a Spanish phrase.

"Habla en ingles," Simmons said.

"¡Fuego!"

Simmons looked up and saw the man holding a jar with a burning fuse. He knew why his friends hadn't fired. If that guy up there falls and that jar explodes, the whole building could go.

Simmons didn't care. He'd rather go down fighting than wait for him to deliver that deadly candle. He reloaded his gun, aimed it into the hole, and pulled the trigger.

The ceiling opened and the man came crashing with it onto the wooden crates. The jar shattered in a blaze of heat and the liquid inside spread across the guns and ammo with the flames dancing on top. It reminded Simmons of a gas fireplace with the perfectly fueled flames, lots of orange and blue.

The man appeared to be dead from the fall but Nelles aimed at him. "Hasta la bye bye."

He shot him twice in the back before helping Simmons and Curtis stamp out the flames. But they couldn't. The more they jumped, the more the flames ignited the grain dust on the floor and walls. The fire was drawing from the breeze off the river and the flames sprung upward toward the broken ceiling. It was as if they were standing in the middle of a chimney and in front of them was at least two hundred pounds of live ammo.

"Let's get the fuck out of here," Simmons said, grabbing one narrow crate. "Help me with this."

Nelles picked up the other end and they carried it to the door.

"Curtis, find the missiles," Simmons said.

He lifted the burning lids off several crates, searching for the right thing, shielding his face from the waves of heat. "This it?" he asked, holding up an object that looked like a small rocket.

Simmons didn't know but it looked close. "Take as much as you can carry."

They dragged the crate with the anti-aircraft rocket launchers outside. Curtis followed with a box of missiles and Simmons was about to go back for more when the first of the crates exploded like firecrackers in a shoebox. Bullets were whizzing around the building and through the walls.

"Too late," he said.

They dragged what little they'd salvaged down to the water. Inside the crate were two heavy rocket launchers that made Simmons's old bottle rocket launcher seem like a plastic toy. They lifted them onto the boat with the ammo and shoved off.

The grain elevator exploded a second and third time as Simmons set the houseboat in gear and turned up river. The concrete walls of the elevator tumbled into the river with a splash, like an Alaskan ice flow. He noticed his hands on the steering wheel were lightly burned, the hair on his arms singed. Curtis and Nelles were already on deck cracking open beers and jabbering about who killed whom.

Simmons kept staring at the article that he'd clipped out of the newspaper he got from Ripper. That reporter from Chanhassen definitely knew something. He'd sent nearly a half dozen e-mails to Kemper but Simmons had received no response. When he got into town, Simmons thought he'd have to contact Sarah Waverly.

The cabin that Strickland had rented from a wealthy unsuspecting doctor, wasn't the largest on Lake Sylvia, but it could easily sleep all ten of the NSA agents. He used the A-frame cabin that was an hour northwest of Chanhassen as the hideaway for Ann Osland and her two sons.

He dialed the video conference phone on the TV set and waited for Candace McKnight to pickup.

"I've made arrangements," she said without greeting him. Her video image kept breaking up. The density of trees around the cabin weakened the satellite signal. "I can have thirty million deposited into his bank account by noon today."

"Make that forty million," he said.

McKnight rubbed her hands over her face. "What? I thought you said thirty million."

"I told you he doesn't care about the money. He'll keep changing the amount to buy himself time."

"We'll make a partial payment," she said. "Thirty million immediately until I get approval for the rest."

"Hold off on the money. I've taken us on another course of action. We searched his home yesterday."

"Were you in the house?"

Strickland watched a fishing boat across the lake chug by with a line in tow. By now, he could use a vacation, too. "We were in briefly but we couldn't find the almanac so we took the next best thing."

"We agreed you wouldn't touch his wife and children."

He waited for a moment, choosing his words carefully. "I had no choice, Candace."

"So help me, if you fucked this up, I'll have you thrown out of the CIA," she said, pointing at him through the TV.

"Don't threaten me with your office politics," he hollered back. "I'm the only one here with enough experience to know what he's doing. Your department hired me to find a resolution to this problem and I am."

She ran her fingers through her short brown hair. "Where are they?"

"Do you really want to know, Candace?" Strickland asked. "Or are you afraid that might implicate you, too?"

"We agreed the family members wouldn't be involved," she said.

"No, you and Brent Turks agreed," he said. "But I'm the one working in the field and I had to adjust the game plan. Osland cares more about his family than he does about the money."

"What did you do with them?!"

"Fuck you, Candace," he said, before pushing the Off button on the remote.

Eddy's attorney, Carl Grady was right, the Honorable Judge Henderson wasn't absorbing all of this very well. She gave Eddy strange looks of disgust as she heard the evidence set before her. Each time the District Attorney, Albert Wards, made a comment, Eddy's Attorney went after him.

"Gentlemen, this is a bail hearing," Judge Henderson said. "A grand jury will review the evidence in this case. We're here to decide whether or not Mr. Osland should be released."

"The state is requesting that he not be released, your Honor," Wards said.

Grady stood up, pounding his fist on the table. "What?!"

Judge Henderson paged through her notes. She seemed just as shocked as Eddy's attorney. "Is the crime committed by Mr. Osland so heinous you're asking that he remain in custody?"

"We're going for murder in the first degree," Wards said.

"But you have no bodies, Mr. Wards," she said. "No murder weapon, and from what I've heard, little motive."

The D.A. lifted a file. "We have evidence."

"Circumstantial evidence," Judge Henderson said.

"Your honor, my client has no criminal history," Grady said, standing over Eddy. "He's a successful businessman and a family man. To say that he's a threat to society is ridiculous."

"I agree," Judge Henderson said, glancing toward Eddy. "I'm releasing you on bail, Mr. Osland."

Eddy watched the D.A. reviewing his notes. For a man who had just been handed a case, he seemed to be well rehearsed.

The D.A. bowed slightly. "Very well, but the state is requesting that Mr. Osland be under a meaningful bail amount," Wards said. "He's a public figure and we don't want to send the impression that we go easy on people like him. Besides, he's an investigative reporter. I'm concerned that he'll snoop around with his own brand of vigilante justice. An amount of $1,000,000 wouldn't be unreasonable."

"I set the bail, Mr. Wards, not you," Henderson said.

"A $1,000,000?!" Grady shouted. "That alone implies guilt. Your Honor, this entire incident is a mistake. My client is innocent. His home was ransacked and he's asking for the state's help to find his family. There's no evidence of murder and I'm concerned we're rushing to justice here."

"Calm down, Mr. Grady. We could get by without your theatrics," Judge Henderson said.

"Your Honor, I have a compromise that I would like to recommend," Wards said. "May we approach?"

Both the prosecuting attorney and Carl Grady approached the bench. They spoke with heated whispers as Eddy sat alone with a single guard standing behind him.

Grady returned and sat next to him. "She'll set the bail at $500,000 but you'll be under house arrest at a hotel," he said. "You can't go anywhere near the crime scene. You can travel from your hotel to work and that's it. You'll have to wear a tracking device on your ankle."

"No," Eddy whispered back, never letting his eyes off the judge. "A tracking device? Whose idea was that?"

"The D.A. recommended it."

"They got to him. This fits their plan. The NSA wants to watch me."

"Take the deal, Eddy."

"No. I'm not wearing a leash. I have things to check out. I don't want them tracking me."

"Is there a problem?" Judge Henderson asked.

Grady smiled. "No, your Honor. I need one more minute." He turned and said to Eddy, "If you refuse the offer, you're only confirming their paranoia," Grady said. "The judge thinks you might run."

Eddy took a deep breath and thought about it. "I don't even know if I have $500,000 in assets. I can't come up with that kind of bail bond. This whole thing is a joke."

"Well, that's the other thing," Carl said. "The D.A. is pissed off. The judge mentioned that somebody called in this morning offering to pay your bail, no matter how high it's set."

"Who?"

"We don't know. The person wanted to remain anonymous."

Tom DeVaney's office at CNN was at the far end of a hallway and when somebody was looking for him he could usually hear the click of their shoes as they walked. He sat behind a mountain of press release drinking a SlimFast chocolate shake, listening to the sound of running shoes gripping the linoleum floors in the hall.

Matthew, the bureau's Webmaster, had an unmistakable sound to his gait, it was an easily identifiable squeaky jog.

"What is it, Matthew?" Tom said without looking up from his news copy.

"How did you know it was me?"

Tom looked up from his paperwork at the young man in blue jeans and Polo shirt. "I had a hunch. That's why I'm a reporter and you're a Webmaster. What can I do for you?"

"Did you get my e-mail?"

Matthew had a reputation for being a non-verbal, almost elusive staff member. He was committed to e-mail and he never spoke to anyone without first sending a letter. The fact that he'd ascended three floors to talk to Tom face to face was significant. Tom glanced at his computer screen. "I'll get to it soon. Why?"

"What's with that story that was posted on the Website?" he asked.

"Which story?"

"The one about the weather," Matthew said, shifting the weight from one running shoe to the next. "I'm overloaded with e-mail from people responding to the story. I forwarded the messages to you."

Tom spun in his chair and opened the e-mail box on his screen. Matthew had forwarded over one hundred messages to him. The descriptions were all similar:

> *"I've noticed unusual weather at my cabin."*
> *"Have video of snow falling in August."*
> *"I believe the weather is controlled, too."*

Tom took a sip of his SlimFast and looked back at Matthew. "How often do these come in?"

"About every two or three minutes I get another batch," he said. "But the e-mail isn't so bad. Have you checked out our Website this morning?"

"No, what's wrong?" Tom said as he opened his Web browser.

Matthew leaned on his desk. "Somebody hacked into our site and sprayed it with graffiti."

Tom pulled up the CNN Website. The page looked normal at first. All the daily headlines and photos were displayed as usual. Halfway down the page, next to Osland's article about the weather, was a graphic of a butterfly flapping its wings.

"Click on that butterfly," Matthew said.

Tom clicked on the butterfly and suddenly Osland's article was the only news story on the CNN site. The butterfly split into two, then multiplied into three and then multiplied again until the entire screen framed the story with butterflies flapping their wings.

"Who do you think did this?" Tom asked.

"I checked the programming code," Matthew said. "They identified themselves as a group called Chaotica."

Mark Barnes walked alongside of Eddy, escorting him out of the courtroom with another police officer. Eddy noticed Strickland behind the crowd of reporters rushing toward him for a photo.

Strickland leaned against a wall, smiling at him. "If you still think you're getting that money, forget it."

"You son of a bitch!" Eddy said, wading through the crowd toward him.

Mark and the other officer pulled Eddy back and the photographers shoved their cameras in for a better photo opportunity.

"Let it go, Eddy," Mark said.

Strickland only smiled, stepped away from the wall, and walked down the hallway.

Mark whisked Eddy out the side door of the building to the squad car parked behind the courthouse, but there was no escaping the crowd of reporters mingling on the steps.

"Get out of his face," Mark said, shoving the cameras back.

Eddy didn't even try to conceal his identity. Everyone in town knew what he looked like anyway. He wanted to stop and answer their questions, but his attorney had warned him that sound bites on TV could make even an innocent person look guilty.

Just as Eddy was about to sit in the squad car, Alex Andrews reached for his arm. "Ozzie, what's this all about?"

"I can't talk to the press, Alex."

"Somebody's setting you up. I know you, Ozzie. You wouldn't kill Ann and the boys. Tell me what's up."

Mark pushed back more reporters as Eddy sat in the squad car.

"I've been advised not to talk about it."

"They're fucking you over because of that almanac, aren't they?" Alex asked.

"Yeah, you could say that."

"The NSA stormed our office yesterday after you left. I'm ready to tell your story."

"Did you pay my bail?" Eddy asked. "Is that why you stopped by here?"

Alex shrugged. "No, I heard an anonymous donor put up the money."

"I thought it was you," he said, looking out at the crowd in the rear window.

"Wish it were," Alex said. "Let me help. I know you're innocent."

"If you want to help, you have to retrieve the almanac and the satellite sensor from the freezer in my house," Eddy said. "Can you do that?"

A dozen black garbage bags had been set in a row inside the Osland's garage and Strickland walked by each one inspecting the evidence. Roy Manning and seven other men and women filtered into the garage. FBI agents hustled in and out of the house as neighbors sat on the curb watching and pointing.

"Have you come across any manuscripts, diaries, or notebooks?" Strickland asked FBI agent Dick Jeffries.

"Mr. Osland mentioned an almanac yesterday," Jeffries said. "But we haven't seen it. Help yourself."

"Very good," Strickland said. "Which of those bags has Osland's reading materials?"

"The one on the end."

Manning ripped it completely open and the team sifted through books and magazines. The agents picked up everything and examined it twice.

"Anything?" Strickland asked.

Manning shook his head. "Negative."

Strickland kicked another bag. "Keep looking."

Out of the corner of his eye, he noticed a man walking toward the front door. Strickland stepped out of the garage. "Excuse me, nobody's home. There's a police investigation here."

When the man turned around, Strickland realized it was that reporter from the TV station, the one Osland had given the fake almanac to.

"Alex Andrews, right?"

"Yes. We meet again," he said, sliding his hands in his pockets playing with the keys.

"Eddy's not home. You should know that or don't you watch the news?"

"Thought I'd stop by and cover the story for tonight's evening broadcast."

Strickland looked across the lawn beyond the police tape at what was probably Alex's Lexus. "Covering the story for the news, huh? Where's your cameraman?"

Alex shifted his weight from one foot the next. "He's running late. He'll be here soon."

"Is there something in the house that you want, Mr. Andrews?"

"No, why?"

Strickland walked over to him and stood within three inches of his clean face and bright white teeth. "Is it your intention to interfere with our investigation?"

"Not at all."

"Then I suggest you leave before I have you arrested," Strickland said.

Alex took two steps back over a shrub. "Alright, be cool."

He walked back to his car and Strickland watched him drive up the road. When the car left the gates of Stone Creek, he called to his team.

"Roy, I want a team to search the house again."

Mark had packed a duffel bag with Eddy's laptop and belongings and reserved a room for him at the Clark House, a Victorian Bed and Breakfast two blocks off Lake Minnetonka. When Eddy handed the owner his credit card, she swiped it through the terminal four times before handing it back to him.

"I'm sorry," she said. "It's not taking your card."

Eddy handed her a different one and after another half-dozen attempts, she smiled back sheepishly. "This one doesn't work either."

"They've cut me off," he said to Mark. "They've shut down my credit, too."

Mark handed the woman his credit card. "I'll cover his bill."

Eddy walked to the window and looked out onto the street. He expected to see a van out front spying on him, but nobody was there. He lifted up his pants leg and examined the heavy tracking device on his ankle.

"No heroics," Mark said. "This is your temporary home. Lynette and I will drop off your truck. You can go from here to work each day and that's it. We'll clear this up in a few days."

"I can't resume my life, waiting for a bogus trial."

"Let the authorities work this out, Eddy. If you run, you'll be a hunted man."

He wasn't about to argue with Mark. He was tired and ready for bed. He picked up his bag and walked up the creaking stairs to his room. His ankle was already sore from the tracking device rubbing against his skin.

The anguish he felt for his wife and sons was making him sick. "When a body is missing, how long do you wait before you hold a funeral?"

Mark looked down at the wood floor and back up at him. "Don't think that way, Eddy."

Eddy walked into his room and closed the door. The room had a large four post bed, a fireplace, and desk in front of the window. He dropped the duffel bag on the bed, set his computer up on the table, and plugged it into the phone jack on the wall.

As soon as he turned the computer on, the e-mail message icon flashed notifying him that he had one hundred and seventy five messages. At least half of the them were marked urgent, and except for one from Mara and Tom at CNN, he didn't recognize the names of the senders. He read Tom's e-mail first:

Eddy,

    We're flooded with responses to the weather story. I've forwarded the letters to you. When will you get me a story I can air on TV?"

                                                              Tom

He was about to write back to his friend and tell him that his legal troubles had him tied up. He would have to hand this over to Alex Andrews. As he scrolled the list of e-mails Tom had forwarded, the descriptions caught his eye:

    "I've seen strange weather in Michigan."
    "Almost always rains on Tuesdays."
    "Read your story. I'm a believer."
    "We had snow in July. I have photos."

People had written to him confirming that they too had suspicions about the weather. Eddy opened each letter and read it from top to bottom. Some of the letters had photos attached such as unusual cloud formations, snow covering very small areas in the off season, lightning striking the same place repeatedly.

    He wanted to write a column about how the government was framing him but he didn't want to sound like a crackpot. And if his family was alive somewhere, he couldn't jeopardize their safety any further. Instead, he forwarded the letters to his editor friends at other newspapers asking them to print a few.

    The last letter he opened was from Mara. It was simply a note of encouragement and when he read it, he began to cry.

Eddy,

    "The dreamers are the saviors of the world. As the visible world is sustained by the invisible, so men, through all their trials and sins and sordid vocations, are nourished by the beautiful visions of their solitary dreamers. Humanity cannot forget its dreamers; it cannot let their ideals fade and die; it lives in them; it knows them as the realities which it shall one day see and know."

Quoted from, As A Man Thinketh, by James Allen.
We believe in you, Eddy. We know you're innocent.

Mara

CHAPTER SEVEN

An honest man and a northeast wind generally
sleep together.

IT WAS 3:30 AM when Eddy gagged on the duct tape wrapped around his mouth. He sat up in the hotel's four post bed with a flashlight blinding him. All he could make out was the silhouette of somebody sitting on his chest.

"Don't make a sound," the woman whispered into his ear.

Eddy heard the creaking of footsteps outside in the hallway and his captor waited for them to pass.

"Are you a murderer, Eddy Osland?" she asked. "Not likely," she said, answering her own question.

His heart raced, he could hardly get enough air through his nostrils. Was this a government spy here to eliminate him? She removed a metal wand from her belt and waved it over his chest, his groin, and his legs. The wand beeped as it glided over his ankle.

"They've got you by the balls, or should I say by the ankles?"

He wasn't sure if he was supposed to respond. He had tape over his mouth. He simply shrugged.

"A couple of days ago," she said quietly. "You were searching for Joe Simmons. Now he's searching for you. Would you like to meet him?"

He nodded, yes.

"He wants to see the almanac."

She ripped the duct tape off Eddy's face with a fast burning pull. She pointed the flashlight up to her own face. "Remember me?"

It took a few seconds for Eddy to place her face. Her long silver and gray hair tucked under the black knit cap. "Dr. Waverly?"

She smiled and climbed off him. "I didn't mean to frighten you, but we can't have you screaming in the middle of the night."

Eddy looked her over. She was dressed in black jeans, a black sweater, and boots. "What are you doing here?"

"I've come to set you free," she said, snapping a large wire cutter from her belt. "Let me see your leg."

He pulled his leg away. "I can't run from here."

"Do you want your family back?"

"My family's dead."

"Maybe and maybe not," Waverly replied, examining the tracking device.

"I appreciate your interest in helping but I've got a reporter friend who can dig around for me."

"Alex Andrews?" she asked. "I had your home under surveillance all day. Trust me, he didn't get his hands on the almanac."

Eddy wiped the rough beard on his face where tape had left its burn. "If I run I'll be in deep shit with the court."

"You're already in deep shit. Besides, it's the least you could do. Simmons posted your bail."

"Simmons bailed me out?"

"He considers you a worthwhile investment," she said. "We don't have a lot of time so I'll make this brief. To clear your name, and to hopefully get your family back, you have to get that almanac to Simmons. Where is it?"

"It's hidden in my house," he said. "But I'm not running."

She clamped down on the ankle bracelet with her cutter and snapped it off onto the floor. "As of right now, they think you *are* running. If you want a way out of this, you'll come with me out that window."

"Ah, hell," he said, jumping out of the bed.

He followed her to the open window and looked out at the gables and the steep roofline. "Why can't we go out the back door?"

"Cops are out there," she said. "It's the window or nothing at all." She stared at him as he looked over the edge. "Come on, I'm thirty years older than you are. If I can scale this roof, you can."

He climbed after her along the steep roofline, slipping on the weathered shingles, before they reached a large branch of an oak tree. Waverly scooted across it first and Eddy followed her, all the while amazed that this was the scientist he'd met at the Arboretum - the one who didn't want to get involved.

They dropped to the wet grass and ran between the buildings to an alley where she had an idling Jeep. They climbed inside, and Waverly looked up at the dark room, the ambient streetlight reflecting off the broken window.

"Now the police and the NSA will be looking for you," she said, driving into the cool morning air.

"What gives the NSA the right to do all this to me?"

They hit a dip in the road and the Jeep sailed right over it. "National security. You're public enemy number one. Congratulations."

"Where are we headed?"

"Back to your house," she replied. "To get the almanac."

"We don't need to," Eddy said. "I had another copy made."

"Where is it?"

"I had it shipped to a Kinko's store in Maui for safekeeping."

"There isn't time," she said. "Besides, we have to make sure the NSA doesn't get their hands on the original. We're going to your house."

"The police will be there waiting for me. You just said the NSA has been camped outside my house."

"I know, I know," she said. "But we need the almanac. Where is it inside the house?"

"In the back of the freezer."

She laughed and hit the steering wheel. "You're joking, right?"

He held on tightly to the bar above his head as the Jeep hit another bump. "No, it's in a Ziploc bag, behind the frozen meat, along with the satellite sensor."

She shook her head. "In the freezer! No wonder they're still looking for it."

Waverly parked the Jeep inside an abandoned barn, in a field on the south edge of Stone Creek beyond a railroad track. She left the keys inside and Eddy followed her across the muddy field toward his neighborhood with the moonlight at their backs. She'd described the plan to him while driving from the hotel and they were still debating the risks.

"The police will be at the house waiting for me," he said again.

"Actually, the NSA will be waiting for you. They drive expensive government-designed vans. You can't miss them," she said sarcastically. "The police are on their way. By now, you know what a squad car looks like."

"And you want me to run up to the house and take the almanac without anyone noticing?"

"Do you have a keypad entry for your garage?" she asked, sliding in the mud as she walked.

"Yeah, I can get in through the garage," he said.

"Then you'll go in from the front. Let them see you and then turn and run," she said. "While you're distracting them, I'll break in from the back and get the almanac."

"That's it? You want me to turn and run?"

"It's a wild goose chase and you're the goose." She pulled her knit cap tighter over her head.

"What if they catch me?"

She picked up the pace, sloshing across the field. "Then I'll look forward to your prison Christmas card every year."

They slid down a grassy bluff and stopped in the middle of the railroad track. Eddy's neighborhood was over the next hill. Waverly removed a lighter from her pocket, lit it and waved it into the night air. Down the tracks another flicker of light waved back.

"What was that, a signal?" Eddy asked.

"I want you to run back here and head north up this track and wait for me to pick you up under the first train bridge," she said.

Eddy examined the railroad track stretching out into the night. The area was wide and flat on either side, sloping off into a ditch. "They could easily follow me in a vehicle through here. How about if I run across the field back to your Jeep?"

"Don't lead them back to the Jeep," she said. "Run on the track and stay in the middle."

He looked down at the uneven railroad ties and jagged rocks. It would be difficult to run on that stuff.

She grabbed him by the shoulders and looked him straight in the eyes. "Assuming you get this far without getting caught, whatever you do, stay in the middle of the track. And run like your life depends on it."

Eddy reached his driveway, ran up to the garage, and punched the code into the keypad. The door opened as if the house were waking with a slow yawn. He scooted under the rising door and saw the entire garage floor covered with plastic bags and his personal belongings. A searchlight from somewhere up the street beamed on him. He reached down, picked up a magazine as if he had the almanac, and ran out of the garage across the yard.

Headlights flashed on and came raging down on him as he crossed the street and ran into a neighbor's backyard. He looked back and saw a van following him. In the distance, he heard police sirens.

Eddy scaled a small hill, slipping on the morning dew, and the van bounced over the curb onto the lawn after him. The headlights swayed back and forth projecting Eddy's image against the backdrop of trees, like the shadow of a prisoner against the penitentiary walls.

Sarah threw a rock through the sliding glass door, chipped away at the chunks of glass, and ran into the kitchen to the freezer. She reached inside, fumbling in the dark, grabbing at frozen waffles, vegetables, and meat. In the back, just as Eddy had described, was a notebook wrapped in cold plastic. Next to it was a box that she assumed was the satellite sensor.

She felt metal pressing against the back of her neck.

"Give it to me," a man said.

The cold air billowed out of the freezer, and she herself, froze with fear. She had never suspected that they'd have somebody inside the house.

"I said give me the almanac," the man repeated.

"Are you vegetarian?" she asked.

"What's that supposed to mean?"

Sarah wrapped her hand around a bag of frozen hamburger and turned swiftly, hitting him upside the head. She heard the gun fall, spinning across the wood floor. The man staggered back and she hit him again across the face.

"That's why I'm a vegan," she said to the man unconscious on the floor. "Meat's hard on your system."

She grabbed the almanac and the satellite sensor and ran out the broken door.

Eddy had reached the railroad track and now the police sirens were louder, only blocks away. He heard the chopper blades of the helicopter sweeping over his neighborhood. The van blazed through the brush, turned, and followed him onto the tracks just as he feared. He sprinted down the middle, stumbling on the rocks and railroad ties, remembering what Sarah had told him, "Whatever you do, stay in the middle of the track."

Strickland slammed on the brakes in front of Osland's house, ran through the garage, and into the kitchen where he found one of his men wiping a bloody nose with a paper towel.

Strickland looked back at the open freezer. He felt like a fool.

"Somebody update me," he said into his headset.

"He has the almanac but we've got him on the railroad track," agent Wentz said.

Strickland ran out onto the deck and watched the helicopter hovering over the house. "I want the bird over the track."

The van was closing in when the helicopter descended low, one hundred yards in front of Eddy. The helicopter hovered with its searchlight, waiting for him while the van narrowed the gap.

Out of the early morning mist, two young men appeared to Eddy in the middle of the railroad track. They were crouched low, blocking the wind from the chopper with their camouflaged shirt sleeves. He heard one of them hollering in a Spanish accent. "Venga Aqui. Middle of the track!"

The van accelerated toward him and the helicopter swiveled as it started to set down. Eddy ran toward the two shadows. Suddenly, both the van and the helicopter lifted off the ground in simultaneous explosions. He looked back to see the van toppling upside down, rolling into the ditch. Ahead of him, the helicopter had tipped over on its blades.

"Run! Ahora!" one of the shadows said.

Eddy sprinted forward again, running through flames, down the middle of the track.

"Joe Simmons?" he said out of breath, approaching them.

The two of them laughed and exchanged a joke in Spanish.

"Curtis and this is Nelles," the smaller one said, leaning on a large tube that looked to Eddy like a bazooka gun.

"Did you blow up that chopper and van?" he asked.

He raised the tube onto his shoulder. "A lo mejor..maybe."

"Thanks, you saved my life," Eddy said. "Where are we headed?"

"The river," Nelles said, shaking a can of spray paint. He bent over and sprayed something on the railroad ties and rock. "Vamos."

The men were climbing out of the van and helicopter with the help of the other NSA agents as Strickland walked the uneven track. On the ground ahead of him, he spotted a document with its pages flapping in the wind. He shined his flashlight on it, and for a moment he felt a sense of relief. Had Osland dropped the almanac? He ran to it and picked it up. It was Sports Illustrated.

"Mother fuck!" he shouted, throwing the magazine in the ditch. He turned his headset on and pressed a button on his belt. "Roy, where are you?"

Roy Manning answered him from only a few yards away. "I'm here," he said, waving his flashlight. "You have to see this."

Strickland jogged the uneven split logs in the center of the track. He passed the helicopter pilot sitting next to the chopper, holding his arm.

He reached where Manning stood and looked down at a logo painted in blaze orange paint on the rock. He recognized the butterfly with a circle around it. He hadn't seen it in nearly thirty-five years.

"The Shaman," he said.

Manning nodded, still pointing his flashlight at the wet paint. "I read about him during my training. He would run through the jungles during the Vietnam war and spray paint that sign on trees and rocks. He was one of the pioneers of the Weather Program, wasn't he? I thought he was dead."

"So did I," Strickland said. He looked around at the wreckage, the flames, and smoke. It all came back to him vividly. During the war, rumors had spread from one platoon to the next that the Shaman could make rain in hills. He was sometimes attributed with making the sun come out just when the American troops needed it the most. For awhile, the legend of the Shaman was nothing but a fable, like the stories of mermaids made up by sailors looking for comfort.

But the signature butterfly began appearing on trees, huts, and roads. And when the weather didn't always work to the Americans' advantage, senior military officials wondered if the Shaman was making a statement of his own. They had a war protestor in the middle of their war.

Strickland himself had spent the better part of the war tracking him. He and two other men risked their lives chasing after that damn logo and now thirty-five years later it had resurfaced.

Eddy, Waverly, Nelles, and Curtis had switched vehicles three times during their escape from Chanhassen. They had left behind the Jeep for a rusted Cadillac, and the Cadillac replaced by a Buick Regal that had no shocks. By dawn, they had reached St. Paul's Mississippi river flats where a sign greeted them: "Third World Yacht Club". Eddy noticed somebody had spray painted below, "Members Only."

The houseboats were lifeless except for a few dogs walking docks, sniffing for food. The river had a musty, oily smell and, because of the high limestone walls on either side, there was no breeze. Eddy looked into the soft gleam of dusty windows. "He lives here?"

"He lives in Louisiana," Waverly said. "He came here to see you."

"You and Joe Simmons are friends. Is that right?" Eddy asked. He remembered the audio tape of the science lecture they'd attended.

"Not friends, lovers," Curtis said. "He's her man."

"Knock it off," Waverly said. "That was a long time ago."

Simmons had the smallest vessel of all the houseboats they had passed. Along the stern, he had plants, empty cases of beer, and a mountain bike locked to a post. On the bow were lawn chairs, a hammock, and an air mattress. A small satellite dish sat mounted on the roof with what looked like solar panels.

"If you don't mind waiting here for a minute or two," Waverly said. "I'd like to speak with him before you come in."

Eddy nodded. "Thanks."

"For what?"

"For helping me tonight," he said, handing her the almanac and the box with the satellite sensor. "For getting involved."

CHAPTER EIGHT

Rainbow toward the leeward, damp runs away.

SARAH WAVERLY KNOCKED twice and entered the cabin. Simmons was sitting at a small table in the boat's kitchenette, holding a mug of coffee. The smell of bacon was in the air. He stood formally, tossing his long brown dred-locks back over one shoulder as she entered.

He'd aged a lot more than her memory of him. In her mind, he was still that skinny college student, the class math geek with a crew cut. He'd filled out and now looked more like a teddy bear squeezed into a rainbow colored tie-dye shirt.

"You made it," he said, moving closer to her. She wasn't sure if he intended to shake her hand or give her a hug. They did a little of both.

Simmons reached for a metal wand on the table and waved it over the front and back of her body. "I can never be too careful," he said, searching for listening devices. "You're clean."

This wasn't how she'd imagined their reunion might be. She'd always thought they'd run into each other at a science conference. "Good to see you again, Joe."

"Been a long time," he said with a long pause. "Where should I begin?"

"Let's start by getting me a cup of coffee." She set the almanac and the satellite sensor on the table.

"I thought you were bringing that reporter."

"He's out on the dock with your minions. I thought we might need a few minutes alone," she said, looking across the houseboat, realizing how small it was. She could easily touch the ceiling without fully extending her arm. One entire wall had gauges and meters; measuring the outside temperature, wind speed, and barometric pressure. Like Kemper, she remembered Simmons always had a fascination for weather. "You dropped out of society for this?"

"I made a difficult decision," he said with a hint of regret in his voice. "It's been a matter of survival ever since."

"Attitudes have changed."

"Really? Have you changed? Do you still hate me for going over there?"

She was silent for a few seconds, thinking of a way to explain the awkward end to their relationship. "I protested the war, not the men who fought it," she said. "You know I don't hate you."

"You broke up with me because I enlisted."

"I didn't understand why you enlisted. At the time, I didn't believe there was a Weather Program. I'm sorry. I know how you must feel."

"How can you know how I feel?"

"People understand what Vietnam veterans went through. I do, too. You can come out now."

"I went AWOL. Attitudes toward cowards don't change."

"You were alone in enemy territory, fighting for the Americans," she said.

"Was I? How can you be so sure who I was fighting for?"

She swallowed the hot coffee quickly. It burned her throat on the way down. "Well, of course. You used your weather equipment to help the American soldiers. Dr. Kemper told me."

"Dr. Kemper didn't know shit. I went over there thinking I could make a difference. I thought my knowledge of math and chaos theory could be applied to the Weather Program to bring a quick end to the war. I thought I could save lives on both sides. But I realized that the Weather Program was intended to be a death weapon and I had contributed to it. I couldn't be a part of something like that. At the start of Operation Rolling Thunder I bolted. Then they turned on me."

"Who turned on you?"

"The Navy, the Marines, the CIA, you name it," he said. "I spent five years running through the jungle trusting nobody. I used the weather technology that I had on the ground to protect myself. Then caught a boat and made my way back to the states. I was as surprised as anybody to have been listed as an MIA."

"By 1972 I heard you were alive," she said. "Why didn't you contact me?"

"You were involved in that radical group Chaotica," he said.

"I started that group because of you," she said.

"I know," he said with a smile. "I recently gave the group free publicity on CNN's Website."

She pointed to the almanac and box on the table. "We've got evidence that the Weather Program is still up and running."

Joe opened the plastic bag and held the almanac up to the light. "This is fucking beautiful, man. You know what this information might be worth?"

She was more concerned about the environment but she guessed. "Millions of dollars I suppose."

"Billions," Simmons said.

"Since when were you motivated by money?"

He leaned against the table and sipped his coffee. "I'm older now, Sarah. Living as a revolutionary hasn't paid well. I'd like to cash in my chips now."

"Excuse me," Eddy said, entering the boat's cabin. He looked taller squeezing through the short doorway. "It's chilly out there."

"Please come in," Sarah said. "Eddy, meet Joe Simmons. Joe, this is Eddy Osland."

Simmons looked him over, slow to shake Eddy's hand. He waved the wand over Eddy's body.

"I've been looking all over for you," Eddy said.

Simmons grabbed the almanac, walked across the room and sat on the couch. "Yeah, you and everyone else."

Alex paced his office with Jason Hurley as he spoke with Tom DeVaney of CNN. The incident he'd missed earlier that morning was now broadcast nationwide.

"A manhunt is underway," Alex said to Tom.

"This doesn't look good," Tom said. "The media is portraying Eddy as a terrorist."

"We both know he's not," Alex said.

"Of course not, but where'd he get the explosives?"

"I don't know," Alex said. "I bet it has something to do with that anonymous bail donor."

He picked up a newspaper with more photographs of the accident scene. Below was another article about Eddy Osland and pictures of his missing wife and children.

"Has he called you?" Tom asked.

Alex turned on his cellular phone and checked his messages. "No, but when he does we'll contact you."

Candace McKnight and Brent Turks were not holding up well under the barrage of questions from The Joint Chiefs of Staff at the Pentagon. For years, the NSA was accountable to nobody, now everyone was breathing down their necks.

At the far end of the conference room was a wall covered with monitors tuned to news broadcasts across the country. McKnight couldn't take her eyes off the pictures of Osland's wife and children. On the long oak table were printouts of satellite images.

"What's with you people?" Secretary of Defense, General Douglas Liden asked. "You have the greatest communications technology ever developed and you can't even find a man running on foot?"

"Our field commander, Craig Strickland, said Osland had an accomplice," McKnight said. "He escaped in a vehicle."

"Who is this accomplice?" General Liden asked.

"Strickland thinks the Shaman has resurfaced," McKnight said.

There was a collective silence amongst the group and McKnight knew they had a million questions that she couldn't answer.

The Chief of Operations for the Weather Program, Kevin Munson, jabbed his pen into a legal pad. "The Shaman's dead."

"Not according to Strickland and I think he would know," she said. "Our NSA agents were led into a classic military ambush. They used anti-aircraft weapons against our men. The Shaman's signature was left behind."

"If the Shaman goes public, that'll be the end of it," Munson said. "You can't discredit him. He helped develop our early technology, our mathematical models were designed around his theories. How did this situation escalate?"

"Strickland made mistakes," Turks said. "He didn't follow protocol."

"He took Osland's family hostage," McKnight said, her eyes passing back and forth from the men's faces to the news coverage on the wall. "He may have killed them."

General Liden leaned his wide forearms over the table toward McKnight. "He took hostages? And he killed them?"

"Possibly, he wouldn't give me a straight answer," she said.

General Liden rubbed the stress off his chiseled face. "This is a huge clusterfuck, Ms. McKnight. We don't kill Americans, remember?"

"I'm not exactly proud of this moment in history," she said. "I'm flying to Minneapolis. I need to talk with Strickland, to find out what happened."

The room was silent for another long moment as the group watched the latest update on CNN. An abandon vehicle had been found in a field and dogs had picked up Osland's scent.

"An American helicopter shot down on American soil," said Air Force General, Charles Simms. "That's damn embarrassing."

"We'll catch him. The entire area is under surveillance," Turks said. "We're studying the satellite images as we speak."

McKnight could see she and her boss had lost their confidence. General Simms bounced a pen on the table. "The satellites are what put us in this situation in the first place."

McKnight was frustrated. This wasn't her battle to fight. "General, it's those satellites that protect your troops in the air and on the ground."

"What I'm saying, Ms. McKnight, is that too many resources have been devoted to the Weather Program," General Simms said.

Kevin Munson sat up erect in his seat. He was an elderly man with alabaster skin, as if he never went outside in the light of day. "Without the Weather Program, how do you plan to invade on a foggy night? Sit in your jets praying for cloud cover? The military would've lost so many more people on recon-naissance missions. We wouldn't be a super power today without the Weather Program, and you know it!"

"That's enough, Mr. Munson," Brent Turks said. "Nobody's questioning the value behind your department."

"Without a doubt, this is a tar baby," McKnight said. "We're supposed to distract people from noticing the weather and now we're wrapped up in it."

"Well how the hell are you going to distract the whole country?" Navy Admiral, Reginal Thornton asked, pointing his thick finger at the wall of moni-tors.

"The media thinks he's a fugitive," Turks said. "That's working in our favor."

"But if he and the Shaman go public with this information," Commander Sullivan said. "What will you do, Mrs. McKnight? Will you sit in front of congress and explain the Weather Program?"

"I'm hoping I won't have to," she said. "Mr. Osland demanded a forty million dollar fee to remain quiet. I've made arrangements to transfer the money to him."

"You just said Strickland has taken his family hostage, maybe even killed them," General Liden said.

"I'm giving Osland the money as gesture of goodwill," she said. "I want to distance us from Strickland. I want Osland to know we're still willing to nego-tiate."

"I don't care how much you pay him. We need the President to authorize troops in the area," General Simms said. "And I don't mean National Guard, I want my men up there."

"Fine, we could use the help," McKnight said. She could feel her boss glaring at her. "I'm on the next plane to Minneapolis."

"We already have the police, the FBI, and NSA tracking Osland," Turks said. "We'll be stepping all over one another."

Secretary of Defense General Liden squinted at the wall of monitors, as if watching the action were painful. "I think we should let the President decide that."

After a brief nap, Eddy woke up to a blinding red sunrise streaming through the windows of Simmons's houseboat and the rich aroma of coffee drifting through the air. Alex Andrews was on TV, standing in front of his house describing the early morning tragedy.

Eddy watched for a minute as the sorted details of his life flashed on the screen. His house was torn apart, they had interviews with staff members from his newspaper, and the pictures of his missing wife and sons were all he could take.

Alex held copies of several daily newspapers across the country that ran Eddy's column. More and more readers were responding to allegations of strange weather.

"Don't pay attention to that," Simmons said, pushing a button on the remote. He turned to the Weather Channel. "Come see what we found."

Eddy poured himself a cup of coffee and sat next to Waverly at the table. On the windowsill were glass jars filled with water and small floating disks. Eddy had noticed them the night before. "Are those weather instruments?"

"Galileo's Thermometers," Simmons said. "They measure the temperature. When the temperature rises, the liquid becomes less dense and the floating glass spheres inside sink. I collect thermometers."

Simmons had the almanac open to the day's forecast. Curtis and Nelles were on the other side of the small cabin sitting in front of the computer. Simmons nodded back at the forecast on the Weather Channel. "The farmer's forecast is accurate."

Waverly handed Eddy a sheet of tables. "We printed this off the internet. We compared Mick's forecasts to what actually happened over the last thirty days. He was only wrong on four of those days - which I think proves my theory that the government can change the weather whenever it needs to."

Eddy watched Simmons fan the pages to the mechanical drawing. "Can you rewire the satellite sensor like he did?"

Simmons nodded. "It's not too difficult. For years, we've known of this very same technique. We could log into the weather database, but we could never maintain the connection. We kept getting logged off."

"How did Mick do it?" Eddy asked.

"Dumb luck," Simmons said. "I think it has something to do with how far north he was. We were always closer to the equator and closer to the satellites. But Mick was farther away and could stay online long enough to download data before they zapped him."

"That's how they killed him?" Eddy asked.

"We think they used a bug zapper," Waverly said.

"What's a bug zapper?" Eddy asked.

"Defense mechanism on satellites," Waverly said.

"NASA maintains the satellites in the atmosphere. They've developed a way of killing flies," Simmons said.

"Flies?" Eddy asked.

"Flies are foreign countries or a farmer, as in this case, attempting to suck data off satellites. NASA can trace the signal back and send a surge of electricity along the data line that drops the fly just like the bug zapper you might have in your backyard," Simmons said.

Eddy sipped his coffee imagining the pain Mick must've felt, "God, what a way to go."

"We think we know what the farmer did, but now we have to try it for ourselves," Simmons said. "The encrypted data needs to be translated. Nelles and Curtis could help us but that probably isn't necessary."

"Why not?" Eddy asked.

"You have to answer a few questions first," Simmons said. He lifted a shotgun off the floor and leveled it at Eddy.

Waverly reached out. "Joe, stop."

Simmons hit her hand down.

"Sure, ask me anything you want," Eddy said.

"What's your angle?"

He looked up the barrel of the gun at Simmons's squinting eyes. "I want to publicize this just like you do. And I want to find out what happened to the Jacobsens and my family."

"Curtis ran a background check while you slept," Simmons said. "You recently came into money."

"Money? What are you talking about?"

"Forty million dollars was transferred to your checking account first thing this morning. Did you blackmail Uncle Sam?"

Eddy was as amazed as everyone else in the room. He never thought the NSA would complete the transaction. "No, I mean, yes I did but I was bluffing."

"You're one hell of a poker player, son."

"I was only stalling for time until I could write my story."

Simmons kept the gun pointed at him. "I should be mad as a wet hen right now. I traveled two days and two nights straight up this river to hit the big time and you beat me to it. You stole my idea, newspaper man."

"I don't want the money," Eddy said, his voice cracked from the stress of trying to convince Simmons. "You can have it."

Eddy could see Curtis and Nelles smiling at each other as if they'd hit the lottery.

Waverly raised her hands slowly, trying to get Simmons to release the gun. "Joe, put the gun down."

Simmons handed her the gun and walked out of the room. "I don't want his fucking money. The deal is off."

A sailboat glided across Lake Sylvia as Strickland paced the cabin, reading field reports from his team members. Over fifty residents in Osland's town had been interviewed, family members, and business associates questioned, but nobody had contact with him. Strickland's rabbit had gone underground and it was time to smoke him out.

His SAT phone vibrated and he knew immediately who it was, even before he saw McKnight's name in the green display. "I'm busy, Candace."

"I had my ass chewed off and handed to me in a meeting at the Pentagon," she said. "I'm flying into Minneapolis this afternoon. You and I need to talk about your role in this investigation."

The last thing he needed was upper management following him in the field. "I'm in the middle of a manhunt. I don't have time for an NSA performance review."

"Craig, you're done," she said. "I'm removing you from the assignment. You've caused enough damage."

"You can't do that."

"I already did," McKight replied. "You took hostages."

"It was the easiest way to discredit Osland and gain access to his home," Strickland said. "And so far, I've been successful. Everybody wants him."

"Do you have the almanac?" she asked.

"I'll retrieve it soon."

"As far as I'm concerned, you've failed," she said. "Give me a straight answer this time. Are the wife and children dead or alive?"

Strickland looked out the window of the cabin to a dock on the edge of the lake. Ann Osland and her sons, along with three of his agents, were fishing.

"Dead," he said to McKnight.

Strickland cut her off and dialed the SAT phone again. He waited, typed in a security code, and waited again for clearance.

On the mountainous Naval island of Mitrah, in the South Pacific, Petty Officer Second Class, Denny Holden approved NSA agent Craig Strickland's security status. Private Holden rubbed his temples, battling another one of his headaches. The air was so thin at the command post, very few soldiers could work longer than a two hour shift. In a half-hour they'd allow him to go back down to sea level.

"Go ahead Mr. Strickland," he said.

"Requesting ground cover."

Private Holden turned to an electronic map of the United States on the wall. Across the map were latitude and longitude markings. The west coast was dry, rain had been scheduled for the heartland region, and the east coast was hitting record high temperatures.

"Your coordinates?" he asked.

Strickland gave him the zipcode and Private Holden zoomed the electronic map over Minnesota with the click of his mouse.

"Hard to bring fog in this time of day," Private Holden said. "I'd have to change the jet stream."

"Have you watched the news lately, Private?"

Private Holden hadn't. The island was four hours behind the east coast time zone. He'd never felt the news on the mainland had any relevance. "No, Sir."

"You know me, Private Holden. I wouldn't make this kind of request unless it was absolutely necessary. I'm chasing a group that could expose the entire Weather Program," Strickland said. "I want ground cover so they can't fly out of Minneapolis."

"That would take major programming. I have to get approval for an unplanned change in the system," Private Holden said.

"Do it!"

Strickland clipped the SAT phone to his belt, took a deep breath, and looked up at a cloudless summer sky. Requesting fog might help him find Osland, but he was hoping it would also slow McKnight down. If he could keep her out of Minneapolis for even a few hours, he might buy himself enough time to retrieve the almanac.

Manning opened the cabin's sliding glass door with a phone in his hand. "Did you authorize that payment of forty million?"

"No, I mentioned it to Candace but I told her it wasn't necessary," Strickland said. "Why?"

"Agent Wentz called," Manning said. "She said she checked Osland's bank account. He has the forty million."

"Why would they give him the money? I have the family," Strickland said, before stopping himself. He realized that Candace McKnight had plans of her own. "That backstabbing bitch."

Eddy watched Simmons monitoring the weather gauges on the wall of the houseboat while Sarah Waverly sat outside with Nelles and Curtis, waiting for the tension to settle down.

"Temperature dropped fast," Simmons said. He looked out the window up at the sky.

Eddy could see he was nervous. "Is that significant?"

"It is if you believe the government controls the weather." He picked up one of the Galileo Thermometers, studying the spheres inside. He looked down at the almanac. "Mick hadn't forecast a cold front. They're up to something, newspaper man. You better take your forty million and run."

Eddy looked out the window at the blue sky beyond the yellow limestone walls. "You've had trouble with the NSA before, haven't you?"

"Yeah, the same people who ruined you chased me all over Asia. I've been running for years," Simmons said.

"What is the NSA?"

"They're responsible for protecting all classified data sent over U.S. information systems. They go to great lengths to make sure those systems are impenetrable. The NSA employs the country's largest team of mathematicians to design cipher systems that protect the integrity of U.S. data and to find weaknesses in adversaries' systems. They work very closely with the CIA."

"Tell me, how screwed am I?"

Simmons's face cracked a smile and he shook his head. "Straight up?"

"Don't hold back. Tell me."

"In the 1980s when President Reagan pushed his star wars initiative, he was priming the American public for truth about the Weather Program. He felt the climate was right and he wanted people to know. The CIA, however, had another plan and one day they pumped up this psychotic named Hinkley. Fed his head with all kinds of nasty paranoia crap and he shot the President. Reagan didn't say a word about the Weather Program after that."

"They shot a President to keep this quiet?"

"Reagan was lucky. They murdered JFK for the same offense."

"Holy Christ," Eddy said under his breath.

"Wish you could give back the forty million now?"

"No, I want to expose this and I need your help."

"You don't want my help. In the government's inner circle, I'm known as the Shaman."

"Why?"

"I was involved in the earliest stages of the Weather Program. I showed them how to make rain. I was known as the rainmaker, the witch doctor, the Shaman. If they found out I was here, they'd kill us both on the spot."

"I'll give you the money, Joe."

Simmons tapped the barometer gauge and sat down on the couch. "I don't take charity, newspaper man."

"Well how do you earn your living on this boat?"

"I'm a hired gun. I get paid to hack into computer systems," Simmons said. "Honest pay for a dishonest day's work."

"Consider this an assignment. I'll pay you to hack your way into the government's weather database. How is that any different?"

Simmons thought about that for a moment, as if he were holding out for something more. "Sorry, not interested."

"Fuck you, then."

"Watch the attitude, man."

"No, fuck you and the boat you road in on," Eddy said, kicking an empty beer bottle toward him. "What the hell did you come all this way for?"

"I came to blackmail the government but since there's so much of that going on, I think I'll drift down river!" Simmons shouted back.

"You didn't come here to blackmail the government. You had another motive. What is it? Sarah?"

He rolled his eyes and combed his fingers through his hair. "Yeah, right. I came here to rekindle an old flame. Shit!"

Eddy saw the same butterfly logo that Nelles had painted on the railroad track tattooed on his forearm. "You're here to set yourself free, aren't you."

"I'm already free as a bird."

"Free as a bird in a rusted cage."

"What's with the metaphors, newspaper man?"

"Nelles painted your tattoo on the railroad track," Eddy said. "You want the NSA to know you're here."

"That's bullshit."

"Is it?"

Simmons stood up and walked across the room to the almanac. He opened it to the picture of the satellite sensor.

"What if I can get you your freedom back?" Eddy said. "No more running, no more hiding out on this boat."

"You can't do it."

"Help me download the data," Eddy said. "We'll get news reporter Alex Andrews to capture it on video and I've got a friend at CNN who will air it. Then we'll bargain for your freedom."

Simmons looked at him. "I have my own video camera. I don't need another reporter on this boat."

"We need a reporter with a legitimate reputation for news coverage," Eddy said. "Let go of your ego and you might walk away from this a free man."

Simmons picked up one of his hand-rolled cigarettes and lit it. "And you'll pay me for my services?"

"Name your fee and I'll pay it."

"Ten million for me, ten for Sarah, ten for you, Nelles and Curtis each get five," he said, as if he'd already run the numbers in his head hours ago.

"It's a deal," Eddy said, shaking his hand.

"Yo, amigos," Simmons called to Nelles and Curtis. "You're taking newspaper man into town to pick up a reporter. Pack the jump suits."

"Cool," Nelles said through the window.

"What's a jump suit?" Eddy asked.

Simmons blew smoke out his nostrils and winked. "You'll see."

CHAPTER NINE

If coffee bubbles in the center of your cup, expect fair weather.
If bubbles flow to the sides of your cup, expect rain. If the
bubbles have no fixed position, weather is in transition.

MCKNIGHT AND TURKS shared a limousine back to Dulles International airport, discussing their limited options. McKnight watched Turks as she stirred the bubbles in her coffee with a straw.

"The Secretary of Defense, General Liden, and I have a late afternoon meeting with the President," Turks said. "As soon as you find the family, dead or alive, I want you to call me."

"What will you say to the President?" she asked.

"He deserves to know about the forty million. General Liden will request permission to send in troops," Turks said, rubbing his hands over his face. "He's expendable, you know."

She was afraid it might come to this. "I know. What do you want me to do when I get there?"

"Run a one-eighty on him."

She looked at her boss, his knitted brow and grayish eyes. A one-eighty was a technique the NSA used only when absolutely necessary. "You sure?"

"Do I look like I'm unsure of myself?" he asked. "Run a one-eighty. Then take the money back."

The meteorologists at WMSP were hustling around the studio checking their computers, and rewriting their daily forecasts. Alex had heard they were surprised by the clouds rolling in from the west. His cellular phone rang and he picked it up, still watching the meteorologists across the office.

"This is Alex."

"It's Eddy."

Alex stepped back and sat in a cubicle, covering the mouthpiece. "Ozzie, what happened?"

"Are you ready to help me publicize this story now?"

"That's what I'm here for," Alex said, cradling the phone against his shoulder. He pulled a pen and pad from the desk. "Where are you?"

"We can't talk long. They're listening," Eddy said. "Get a cameraman and drive east on 35E in one of your WMSP mobile news vehicles."

"And?"

The line disconnected.

Strickland and Manning had already parked at the far end of the WMSP lot, waiting for Alex to move. Strickland removed his headphones, pleased that they were back on track. When he ran into Alex at Osland's house the day before, he knew they were working together.

"Did you trace Osland's call?"

Manning shook his head. "Too quick."

"You've got Andrews's cellular number locked in?"

Manning chewed his gum, snapping bubbles. "Any call he makes or receives, rings here as well."

Strickland slipped on his headset to speak with his team members. "Alright, ladies and gentlemen. We're back in business. Our latest target is Alex Andrews, a reporter for WMSP TV. Roy will e-mail you a photo and a bio. Andrews is about to meet up with Osland and possibly the infamous Shaman. We'll be heading east on interstate 35E. I want all teams stationed up and down that corridor. I'll lead."

Strickland turned on the defrost to clear the moisture off the windshield, when he realized it was dew from outside. He opened the window and watched as a thin layer of fog began to sink. It was like a heavy cloud had decided to sit and take a rest over Minneapolis. Things were finally going his way.

Alex pulled Jason Hurley out of a meeting and explained what Eddy had told him on the phone. They ran into the studio where Alex sat behind a desk, combing his hair. He had the story he'd been searching for.

Jason trucked the camera to a tight position. "Ready when you are."

Alex sat up and looked straight into the lens. "Eddy Osland, the fugitive, has agreed to an exclusive interview with WMSP, tonight at ten."

They recorded three more promotional spots before he unclipped his microphone. "Good enough. Tell Dave to run the promos in every commercial break. I'll meet you outside in the van."

The drive from Minneapolis to St. Paul was slow going. The fog had thickened and Alex could barely see more than a car length ahead as he drove the WMSP van. Jason was next to him in the front seat, snapping on a battery to the video camera.

"Where will we meet Eddy?" Jason asked.

"He didn't say. His instructions were to drive east," Alex explained.

His phone rang and he picked it up while driving with one hand on the wheel. "Yeah?"

"It's me again," Eddy said.

Alex squinted through the windshield at the blur of headlights and taillights in the fog. "I'm on 35E. Now what?"

"When you get to the river bridge, you'll see a Buick on the shoulder with its hazards on," Eddy said. "Stop there and we'll pick you up."

"Damn it," Strickland said to himself, weaving through traffic.

He could plainly see on his GPS where he was in relation to Alex's van, but the fog made visual contact impossible. Manning relayed the cellular call to him and the other teams as he drove.

"At the river bridge they're making a switch to a Buick," Manning said.

"We're almost on top of them," Strickland said into his headset. "Follow our lead."

Eddy, Nelles, and Curtis were already on the shoulder of the bridge when the WMSP van eased to the side of the road behind them. Eddy watched Alex and Jason hurry out of the van running alongside of traffic in the mist.

He shook Alex's hand and nodded to Jason. "You two ready for the story of your life?"

"Show us what you got," Alex said.

Curtis opened the trunk of the Buick. "No time for talk, hombres. Put on a jump suit. We have to get down to the boat."

Curtis handed Nelles what looked like a backpack. Eddy wasn't sure what was happening. "Is that a parachute?"

"Sí," Nelles said, strapping on his. "We base jump, man."

Eddy looked over the edge of the bridge. He couldn't even see the river through the fog. "We're not jumping down to the boat!"

"Yeah, we are," Curtis said. "We got NSA up our asses. The boat is below us."

"This is crazy," Alex said, peering over the edge. "We could be killed."

"You stand here any longer," Nelles said, scaling the bridge railing. "I guarantee it."

Eddy was now very aware of the wind and fog as he slipped on his backpack.

Curtis wrapped Jason's camera in bubble-wrap and a plastic bag. "I'll carry the camera," he said.

"I'm afraid of heights," Eddy said.

"We're all afraid of heights," Curtis said. "Just do it, man."

"Over the edge," Nelles instructed.

Eddy climbed over, with Alex and Jason following him in a rush to snap on their packs. He was rigid with fear and gripped the rail tightly, even though he could not see the bottom.

"After you jump, count to three and pull the cord," Nelles said. "When you hit the river, take off the chute or you could be pulled into the river's . . . "

Nelles paused and looked at Curtis as if he couldn't translate the word he had in his Cuban head.

"Undertow," Eddy said. "You could be pulled into the river's undertow."

Nelles snapped his fingers. "¡Sí!"

Eddy held tighter. He could see Jason was white with fear.

"I'm not a good swimmer," Alex said.

"The packs float," Curtis said. "Joe will pick us up in the river."

"Spread out," Nelles said. "I count to three, and you jump, no? Curtis and I follow."

Eddy inched away from the others, still clinging to the railing with the wind at his back. He looked back and saw motorists stopped on the bridge, watching.

Nelles hollered. "Uno! Dos! Tres!"

Eddy didn't move and he realized Alex and Jason hadn't either. He looked over at Nelles and Curtis standing on the bridge railing.

Curtis pointed up the freeway, yelling. "NSA!"

Eddy turned to see at least a dozen men running around the parked cars, across the bridge. Several of them had guns raised. On the limestone cliffs, were more people moving into position. Nelles jumped in a swan dive and disappeared into the fog. Curtis followed, holding the camera, screaming with joy.

"Eddy, I've got a wife and daughter at home," Alex said. "Tell me this story is worth it."

Eddy thought about Ann, Matthew, and Michael. "It's worth it, Alex. Jump!"

"I can't do it," Alex hollered.

"Here they come," Jason said.

"On the count of three," Eddy shouted to Alex and Jason. "One, two-"

Jason went first and Alex followed him. It took a gun shot to move Eddy off that bridge and he jumped into the rushing wind and veil of white. In the free fall, his stomach rose into his chest so fast he could barely breathe. He immediately pulled the cord and was yanked upward by the chute before gliding through wet vapors above the river.

The chute had opened but he felt he was falling much too fast. He looked up and realized the lines were tangled, the chute hadn't fully deployed. He tugged hard on the lines but they wouldn't unwind. He was still in a sloppy free fall with the chute spinning above him like windsock.

He could hear the voices of Nelles and Curtis echoing off the limestone. Below him, Alex's scream of terror stopped as he hit water.

Eddy pulled and pulled on the lines climbing up them. It was as much an effort to avoid the inevitable impact as it was to open the chute. Then, the fog opened and he heard the rushing river.

The current slapped him hard in the chest and he struggled underwater, reaching for the clip to untie his chute. He bobbed up for air and back down again, the rush of cold brown water yanking him under.

He couldn't believe what he had just seen. Strickland stood over the bridge railing, gazing down into nothingness. He could hear them screaming Eddy's name, but he couldn't see them.

Manning spit over the edge. "Who is this guy, Superman?"

"They're below the bridge," Strickland said to other men and women congregating there in awe. "Regroup. Get down there."

The teams scattered off the bridge and Strickland joined Manning at the trunk of the Buick. "This just keeps getting better and better."

"What's next?" Manning asked.

"Where's the team that has Osland's family?"

"They're on the way."

"Good," Strickland said, staring into the fog. "We'll make Eddy Osland come to us."

The houseboat cut through the fog and drifted close to Eddy where his chute had snagged a tree trunk. A very wet and excited Alex cut the lines and helped him onboard. Jason was wrapped in a towel, Nelles and Curtis were shirtless, popping open beers.

"We did it, Eddy," Alex said.

Eddy looked up at the arched metal scaffolding of the bridge. He knew they were all lucky to be alive.

"That was the craziest thing I've ever done," Eddy said.

"I wish I would've had the camera rolling," Jason said. "You should've seen the look on your face, Alex."

"Hey, what about you?" he said.

Eddy noticed Curtis rolling his eyes. "Base Jump virgins."

"Fucking awesome, no?" Nelles said,

"Shut the hell up," Simmons said from the helm of the boat. He was navigating around another sandbar. Sarah was next to him with binoculars, watching the cliff's edge.

"Where are we going?" Eddy asked.

"Down river to find safe harbor," Joe said.

McKnight's plane had circled the Minneapolis-St.Paul International airport for a half-hour waiting for permission to land. The unexpected fog had air traffic backed up in cities all over the Midwest. When the plane had taxied to the terminal she turned on her SAT phone and called Strickland but got no answer.

She speed-dialed the next agent on assignment as she waited to deplane.

"Agent Wentz."

"It's Candace."

"Ms. McKnight."

"Wentz, where are they?"

"Mr. Strickland is at the river. By downtown St. Paul."

"And the family, dead or alive?" Candace asked.

"Alive, of course."

"Where?"

"They're here in one of the vans along the river."

"Give me directions from the airport."

Brent Turks hated to interrupt the President's dinner, but there was no avoiding it. The Secretary of Defense, General Liden, needed the Commander in Chief's permission to take action. And Turks knew General Liden wanted him there to take most of the blame. He brought Kevin Munson from the Weather Program along for color commentary.

By now, even the President was watching the drama unfold on a monitor mounted above the fireplace. The fugitive from Minnesota had made contact with another reporter and the promotional spots about Alex Andrews's upcoming exclusive interview with Osland, was making headlines of its own. Other TV stations were interviewing motorists who were on the bridge and witnessed five people jumping with parachutes. On a coffee table were newspaper clippings of Osland's column.

The President probed his mouth with a toothpick, staring at the news broadcast. "I had two near perfect terms in office. I have six months to go, General Liden."

Turks stood silent, watching the two men talk.

"I know, Sir," General Liden said.

"I'm a lame duck," the President said. "I'm supposed to be in the autumn of my presidency."

"Yes, Sir," General Liden said.

"Then why did this happen?"

General Liden motioned to Turks. "I think he can answer that for you."

Turks stepped forward and stumbled his way through what felt like ten minutes of vague explanations and bullshit. He didn't know how the farmer breached security and he didn't know what was in the almanac.

Kevin Munson finally interrupted him, shaking his tapered finger. "Do you know how important the Weather Program is? Our efforts impact every living thing on the planet."

The President sighed and chewed his toothpick. "Kevin, stop! The Weather Program has been the Pandora's Box of every administration. I'll be damned if I'm the President that gets caught holding the shit bag."

"We could have Special Teams mobilized in the area within the hour," General Liden said.

"If the Shaman comes forward, what will I say to the American people?" the President asked. "What will I say?!"

"We can tell them that the group is involved in terrorism," Turks said. "They've already bombed a vehicle and a helicopter."

"That's why we need troops in there," General Liden said. "Let's get the job done."

The President nodded and flipped his toothpick around so the gnawed end hung outside his lip. "But how will you cover all of this up?"

"We've scheduled a one-eighty, Sir," Turks said.

The President looked over at Turks. "Shoot to kill, gentlemen. Don't miss."

Turks nodded, watching the sterile look on the President's face.

"I want the best sharpshooters you got, General," the President said. "Let's make sure he doesn't walk away from this."

The fog thickened like a wall of smoke around the houseboat, making it difficult to navigate the murky waters of the Mississippi. Eddy could see an island out the window that had an inlet. Simmons seemed to be steering them toward it.

"I'm taking us over there," he said. "Out of the wind, so we can videotape without the boat rocking."

Simmons leaned on the throttle and accelerated across the choppy wake, and the boat's front end lifted slightly.

A rush of water engulfed Eddy's feet. "What's this?"

"Oh, small leak," Simmons called back. "The boat swallowed too many bullets on the trip up here."

Eddy slopped through the water and sat with Sarah, Nelles, and Curtis at the kitchenette table. They had Simmons's computer booted up and they were studying the mechanical drawing in the almanac. Alex and Jason were across the room testing the video camera to make sure it survived the high dive off the bridge.

Within a few minutes Simmons had tied the boat to a tree in the inlet and joined them after checking his weather gauges on the wall. "They're fucking with us, Eddy. Mick hadn't forecast fog for today."

Eddy looked at the dense fog beyond the window where the collection of Galileo Thermometers stood. "How do they change the weather?"

"They might be using a Tesla coil," Waverly said.

"What is it?" Eddy asked.

"It's basically a high-frequency, high-voltage transmitter," Simmons said. "A scientist named Nikola Tesla had invented the device back in the early 1900s to send electricity without wires. The Tesla coil would be an easy way to heat the ocean and atmosphere."

"What bothers me is that there are risks to what they might be doing," Waverly said.

"What she means is, that if the government relies on satellites and a coil to control the weather, then any time a satellite malfunctions the weather could become unmanageable."

Waverly nodded. "That's the danger of relying on chaos theory. It would be like letting a wild tiger out of its cage. You could get it back in eventually, but at what cost?"

"Thirty-five years ago I would've argued that point," Simmons said. "But she's right. There's a huge downside to all of this."

Eddy watched Nelles sitting on the edge of the table reading a diagram, tapping his feet against his friend's chair.

Eddy turned a page on the almanac resting on the table. "Curtis, what do these numbers mean?"

He glanced at the page. "Geo codes."

Simmons nodded. "Latitude and longitude points."

"Makes sense," Waverly said. "If Mick were tracking satellites, he'd need to know where they were in the sky."

"These are geo codes all over the world," Curtis said. "Not just over Minnesota."

Alex was still testing the camera with Jason, listening in. "Why was he concerned about global weather?"

"Who knows?" Nelles said.

"I think we have enough stuff here," Curtis said.

"Can you wire it to meet the specifications on that drawing?" Eddy asked.

"Does the Pope shit in the woods?" Nelles said, lifting the modem into the light. He and Curtis worked diligently, snapping wires.

Curtis studied the programming language on the screen. "We wrote the code for breaking the encrypted data. You can thank Fidel Castro, the next time you see him, for teaching us everything we know."

"How long will this take?" Waverly asked.

"How would I know?" Curtis said. "I never done it before."

They all waited silently, as Curtis held the satellite sensor and Nelles twisted wires. Eddy could hear a breeze blowing through the trees on the island.

Jason turned on the light from the video camera and Alex rehearsed one of his opening lines. "Can the government control the weather? One area resident has proof - damn, let's try that again."

McKnight reached the riverbank where the NSA teams had spread out in groups of two, searching for anyone who might not have survived the jump. All they found were parachutes and packs floating in the water.

She approached Roy Manning and startled him with her voice. "Where's Craig Strickland?"

He slipped in the mud as he turned. "Ms. McKnight, when did you get here?"

"About four days too late I'd say."

"We almost had them. We were this close," he said, pinching his fingers together.

She looked down at the dripping pack at his feet. "Too bad you weren't wearing a chute, too. Maybe you would've caught them."

He dusted off his hands, brushing by her when she grabbed his arm. "Where are Osland's wife and children?"

"Is that why you're here?"

"I specifically told Strickland no hostages."

Manning shook his head. "You what?"

"I told him no hostages."

Manning shifted nervously. "He said you authorized the abduction of the wife and children."

"That's a lie. And if you helped him, you're just as guilty of kidnapping as he is," she said. "I'll send you to prison, Roy."

Manning glanced around, as if he were looking to toss the blame to one of his team members, but he was there alone in the haze. "I was taking orders."

"Tell me right now," she said. "Where are they?"

"Ah, damn it, Candace."

"I want them out of this unharmed," McKnight said. "Where he's keeping them?"

"Down river about a quarter mile," he said. "In one of our vans. He wants to trade them for the almanac."

McKnight left Manning on the riverbank and ran down river where NSA vans were parked just beyond a police barricade. She pushed her way into a crowd of reporters and flashed her identification to get around an Army officer standing under a rain tarp. On the cliff, she could barely see other military personnel in the fog standing with guns.

Strickland was directing his teams and talking into a headset as she approached. "Who invited you to the dance?" he said, staring her down.

"Give them to me."

"Osland and the Shaman are on a houseboat about a half mile down river," he said. "I have them covered."

"Where's his wife and kids?" she asked. "No bullshitting me this time."

"In a safe place nearby," Strickland said. "I'll pull them if I need them."

"You won't need them. Let them go now."

"Is that why you flew out here, Candace?" he asked. "To rescue Osland's family? Whose side are you on?"

"You deliberately disobeyed my orders."

She watched him walk away.

"I'm busy. I've got military and police units stationed up and down the bluff. We can have this chat after it's over."

"Don't you walk away from me, Mr. Strickland," she said. "You're fired!"

"Okay, ordinarily the sensor sits on top of the tractor and relays information inside the cab," Curtis said, straightening in his chair. "But I'll connect the sensor directly to this computer."

"Then can you download the data like Mick did?" Eddy asked. He desperately wanted to capture this on tape.

"We think so," Curtis said.

"Remember, going live is dangerous," Simmons said. "That's how Mick died. You won't get any friendly warnings. If you have any hesitations say so."

"Go live," Eddy said.

"No problem," Curtis said, typing on the keyboard.

Nelles reached for the keyboard. "Dame un chancecito." "Let me take this one."

"Ni se te ocurra, caballón," Curtis said, scooting closer to the desk. "This is a no-brainer."

Nelles yanked on his friend's ear. "Let me, you dweeb."

"You had your chance to break into MicroSoft," Curtis said, holding the keyboard tighter. "Está en mis manos."

Nelles sat in his chair, his arms crossed. "Faggot."

"¡Mamamela!"

Sarah rested her hands on Curtis's shoulders. "Would you please-"

"Here's how this works," Curtis brushed her hands away. "I dial into the same network Mick used for his farm. When I say so, Nelles will move those wires in the sensor like a switch, and we should be able to download classified data Mick downloaded. Then we translate the encrypted data."

The two computer thugs worked together, occasionally nodding to each other as Curtis typed. As long as they were focused on a task, they weren't bickering.

"We're live," Nelles said, watching the monitor.

Curtis typed, paused, and typed again. "Okay, set the switch, por favor."

Nelles moved the wires slowly.

Curtis's face was illuminated from the computer monitor. "Yeah, I'm downloading data."

Eddy watched them working together, reading the data on Mick's computer. "Are you capturing this on tape, Jason?"

Jason gave him the thumbs up sign and Alex stood in the foreground narrating what he saw. Nelles pointed to a string of code, read the almanac, and Curtis nodded and began typing. Occasionally they both sat back from the glow of the computer, as if they were in the presence of greatness, and then leaned in close to the monitor again.

"Fantastico! We're eating through encrypted data like cotton candy," Curtis said. "We're logged into a database."

"What do you see?" Eddy asked.

"The forecasts go out about twelve months. Look," Curtis said.

Everyone crowded around the desk and computer. Eddy could see the tables and graphs.

"Damn. All you have to do is pick a date and a geo code anywhere on the globe, and you'll have your forecast," Simmons said.

"So the source of the weather is the United States?" Sarah asked.

"Sí," Curtis said, reading his laptop. "But they relay all over the world. They call it ARC."

"ARC?" Simmons asked. "What is it?"

"I'm working on it," Curtis said.

Eddy noticed the computer making a series of beeps like a microwave oven that had just finished heating a meal.

"You're getting a warning," Simmons said, pointing at the screen. "Somebody's bulldogging you, hombre. Step down."

"I need more data to figure out who ARC is," Curtis said.

"Listen to him, Curtis," Nelles said. "You don't have much time."

"We're almost there," Curtis said, not moving his eyes from the screen. "I'm downloading a graphic file. Must be a picture."

"Very interesting, but watch your time," Simmons said, louder.

"I got it!" Curtis said. "Here's the logo for ARC."

Eddy leaned in closer and recognized it. "The American Red Cross?"

A blue dot, no larger than a quarter, appeared on the back of Curtis's forehead. At first Eddy thought the dot might be a tattoo he hadn't noticed before, but he realized it was from a light source. He looked up and saw a thin, blue beam of light coming from the ceiling.

"What the hell is that?" Eddy asked. He knew it was coming from outside the boat, maybe from the satellite itself.

Simmons approached the thin beam of light without touching it. "Jesus! Log off! You're out of time, Curtis!"

Alex waved to Jason. "Keep taping."

Waverly stepped back, in shock as if she couldn't form her words. "Bug zapper?"

"Yeah," Simmons said. "They're sighting their target before they zap it."

"A few more bytes," Curtis said, ignoring them, wiping his perspiring head. "Why is the government sending its weather data to the American Red Cross?"

"Everybody get away from the desk," Simmons said.

Nelles looked back at the group. "¿Por que?" When he noticed the blue beam, he screamed, "¡Dios Mio!"

"Que?" Curtis asked, turning to look when the blue dot centered on his forehead. He jumped from the chair to his feet and ran across the room, his feet splashing in the puddles on the floor. "Nelles! Joe! What do we do?"

From the edge of the river, Candace McKnight watched the blue laser slice through the white haze. She looked around to see the other military personnel watching as well.

"Don't do this," she said to Strickland.

He waved her away, talking to somebody in his headset. "You've got the boat locked on target. Destroy it."

"No!" McKnight shouted, reaching for Strickland's headset.

"You're not authorized to kill," she said into the microphone, fumbling with the headphones.

"What are you doing?" Strickland asked, wrestling with her for the headset.

She drew a gun from her raincoat and pointed it at his head. "I already told you, the NSA no longer requires your services, Mr. Strickland."

He raised his arms, stepping back. "They're as good as dead anyway, Candace."

"Not if I can help it," McKnight said, before speaking into the headset. "Power down."

A young man on the other end sounded confused. "They're stealing data."

"Power down," she said again, looking up at the thin blue beam in the sky. "Those are civilians on that boat."

The beam of light followed Curtis, centering on his forehead.

"Subuso," Nelles said, trying to get the group to shut up.

"I'm hot. I'm burning up, man!" Curtis said.

"I feel a vibration," Alex said.

"What's happening?" Waverly asked.

"He's a leech, and they've got him locked on target," Simmons said.

"How? He's nowhere near the computer," Eddy said, watching Curtis hiding in a corner.

Nelles banged the keyboard. "¡Cajones! How do I log off?"

"Don't ask me to explain it," Simmons said. "I've only read about these things, but I've never seen one. It's a tracking device from a satellite."

Jason looked up at the cracks in the ceiling. "We should get out of this boat."

"Keep the camera rolling, Jason," Alex said.

Curtis screamed, "Don't go!"

Joe stood next to Nelles at the computer. "What's taking you so long? Log him off."

"I can't," Nelles said, looking back at his friend.

"Nelles! Help me!" Curtis shouted.

Above the table on the shelf, Eddy noticed the Galileo Thermometers vibrating, the small disks inside colliding into each other, and sinking to the bottom of the glass. The room was heating up. The wet floor beneath their feet also began trembling. Nelles stopped typing and looked around the room, his mouth open in awe. The vibrations increased. The boat was rocking side to side.

"The vibrations are getting stronger," Waverly said.

"I don't believe it," Simmons said, staring at the weather gauges on the wall.

"What? What's going on?" she asked.

The rumbling increased, and the Galileo Thermometers toppled off the shelf one after another, crashing onto the table. Shards of broken glass burst into the air, leaving stains of wet ink on the almanac. The boat shook with such force the support beams cracked and splintered.

"They're using the Tesla Coil," Simmons said.

"What about it? What's happening?" Eddy asked.

"The coil is a high-powered radio transmitter," Joe said, gripping the desk as he spoke. "They use it to charge the atmosphere and alter the weather. This is how Mick Jacobsen died. They tracked him with the satellite, and they used a transmitter and radio waves to charge the atmosphere in the cornfield."

"I'm logged off," Nelles said. "No comprendo. Why is it still tracking Curtis?"

"They know we're here," Joe said. "They're tracking us. We have to break the connection."

A ringing sound pierced Eddy's ears as a beam from the ceiling loosened, knocking him and Joe Simmons to the floor. Bits of wood paneling splintered and rained down on them. Eddy could hardly see anything except the blue beam against the white dust. Simmons crawled across the wet floor under the desk, yanking on cords. He unplugged the computer and the modem, but the beam of light still followed Curtis as he wedged himself between the wall and couch.

"Joe, your electrical box?" Nelles asked.

"In that closet."

"Kill power to the boat," Nelles said.

Simmons splashed to the closet but it was locked. He ran to the next room, searching for the keys. He returned with an axe and hacked his way into the wood door.

"Am I gonna die?" Curtis asked.

Nobody said a word. They held their balance in the boat, staring at Curtis and back up at the blue light penetrating the roof of the boat.

"You're not going to die, Curtis. Hang in there for a minute," Eddy said, trying to comfort the kid.

He seemed much younger, more innocent, than before. He trembled on the floor. His head flipped back and forth. Curtis could no longer form words. "Ahhhhhh!"

Simmons swung the axe at the closet door again and broke a hole wide enough to slide his arm through. The lights went out and the boat was filled with darkness except for the blue beam still plunging through the ceiling.

"Damn it! It didn't work," Simmons shouted.

Curtis screamed again. "Joe! Por Favor!"

CHAPTER TEN

Look for foam on a river before a rain.

MCKNIGHT RAN ALONG the banks of the Mississippi. A frothy foam of brown water lapped up on her shoes as she searched for the boat docked off the island. Military Jeeps had already parked along the water's edge and troops were in position on the bridge above. She realized Strickland had slipped away while she was searching for the boat.

"Disengage your weapon," she screamed into the headset.

"I was given orders by Mr. Strickland to engage the enemy," the Private said.

"Mr. Strickland reports to me. He no longer has authority in this matter," she said. "Don't ruin your career, Private. If you kill a boatload of American civilians, you'll be court-martialed no matter who gave you the order. Disengage!"

Instantly the light vanished and the boat was dark. For a moment, Eddy thought the coil had finished Curtis off and disappeared. He walked over to the couch and touched the young man's sweaty arm expecting soft, crushed bone.

Curtis sat up on his own. "What happened?"

"I don't know," Simmons said. "Somehow we broke the connection."

"You okay there, hombre?" Nelles asked.

"I live! ¡Cajones! I live!" Curtis said, jumping up from the floor.

"Awesome, man," Nelles said, patting his friend on the back.

Jason shined the light from the video camera on Curtis. "You alright?"

"Sí," Curtis said.

Eddy pulled Sarah and Joe aside. "What did Curtis mean about the American Red Cross?"

"It looks like they're broadcasting the data Red Cross facilities around the world," Waverly said.

"But why?" Eddy asked.

Joe threw the power switch back up, ignoring Eddy's question. "We have to keep moving. They know we're here."

He ran up a flight of stairs and turned the ignition in the boat. The engine roared back to life, chugging on the water.

Eddy followed Waverly outside as she untied the boat. "Why would the government give the Red Cross weather data?" he asked.

"Collateral damage would be my guess," she said.

"Elaborate," Eddy said.

"The weather is very dynamic. You can only control the weather for so long before you make a mistake in your calculations," she said. "A snowstorm here, a flood there, and you've got what we call collateral damage. It's a side effect. That would explain why we still have natural disasters - they have defects in their system."

Sarah tossed the rope onto the bow and walked back in the cabin. He followed her trying to get more information. "How is the Red Cross involved?"

"The Red Cross is probably their cleanup crew. They're notified when a disaster is about to hit so it can be cleaned up quickly."

Alex picked up his microphone. "This is great stuff. Can you say that again on camera?"

"I don't think so," she said, wiping the broken glass off the table. "Right now we have to get you to a safe drop-off place so you can air that story."

The boat's engine whined and the craft swerved left, knocking everyone onto the floor.

"Damn it all!" Simmons shouted from the helm. "We got company!"

The houseboat took another hit from the portside and Eddy looked out the window to see Strickland in a large tugboat next to them.

"Heads down," Joe said. "They got guns."

The houseboat ripped through the choppy wake and Simmons kept wiping the moisture off the windows. Eddy held tightly to the table. For a brief while, the houseboat outran the tugboat but gradually the larger craft gained on them and rammed the stern.

Alex and Jason positioned themselves close to the window, trying to capture the footage on tape. Curtis and Nelles joined Simmons up at the helm, helping him navigate in the fog.

"This is it," Eddy said to Sarah. "They're coming for the almanac."

"And once they see Alex and Jason's videotape, they'll want that too," she said.

Eddy held the table tighter as the tugboat rammed them again. "I'm not ready to give up the almanac yet."

Sarah was looking over his shoulder, out at the tugboat swerving at them. "I wouldn't be so sure about that. Look!"

He turned and through the dew on the window he saw the faces of Ann, Michael, and Matthew inside the tugboat. Strickland shouted into a bullhorn.

"My god! Ann!" Eddy shouted.

His sons had caught sight of him and jumped up and down in the tugboat. When the two boats collided again, they fell into their mother's lap.

"What's he saying?" Eddy asked, pushing open the window as Jason pointed a camera at him.

Eddy ran up to the helm where Simmons, Nelles, and Curtis were navigating the houseboat. "Stop. They have my family."

"It's a trap," Simmons said. "Look around you on the cliffs, on the shore. Feds are everywhere. We're not making a deal here."

"Ann and the boys are alive. They're on that boat. Slow down."

"Not here," Simmons said. "It's too dangerous."

The chopper blades from the Airforce helicopter spun overhead and McKnight ducked instinctively, running underneath them.

"I'm coming with you," she yelled to the pilot and sharpshooter inside.

"Sorry, this is for military personnel," the pilot shouted over the wind from the blades.

"Oh, go to hell," McKnight said, flashing her identification. She climbed inside the chopper that had no doors, and strapped on a seatbelt.

Both men were staring back at her.

She shook the rain out of her hair. "What are we waiting for?"

The chopper lifted off the ground, twirling side to side in the wind, and then turned sharply as it flew over the river. McKnight searched the water and shoreline for Strickland. They hovered low above the current, sweeping back and forth, searching for the boat.

"Two boats ahead," the pilot said.

The sharpshooter moved to a new position on the right side of the aircraft and eyed the boats with the scope on his gun.

McKnight leaned to the side for a better view of the tugboat. She recognized Strickland and three other NSA agents onboard. She saw a woman and two young boys sitting in the boat's small cabin.

"Whoa! Wait a minute," she said. "Stop that tugboat."

The pilot looked back at her. "They're with us. It's the houseboat we want."

"Civilians are on that tugboat," she said. "I want them."

The pilot radioed his commanding officer for further instruction. "I've got orders to go after the houseboat."

"Not until you get those civilian hostages off that tugboat," she said, removing the gun from her raincoat.

The sharpshooter raised his rifle at her and McKnight cocked her gun pointing it at the pilot. "You shoot me, I shoot him, and we crash."

"Do what she says," the pilot said.

The sharpshooter lowered his rifle and took off his sunglasses, as if he wanted a better view of her.

"I want the family off that boat, now."

The pilot circled back over the river allowing the houseboat to cruise out of sight around an island. The chopper approached the tugboat head-on.

The pilot spoke into his radio headset, his voice echoing outside the chopper. "Pull over."

Strickland was twenty feet below, blocking the wind from the chopper, waving them off.

"Tell him to stop or you'll shoot," McKnight said.

The pilot repeated her words and the tugboat slowed in the water, moving only as fast as the current.

"Can you lower me onto the boat?"

"We're too heavy," the Pilot said.

"Then get us as close as you can," McKnight said.

"We lost them," Simmons said.

Eddy looked up the river unable to see around the last bend. He was glad to see his family was actually alive. "Why did that helicopter stop them?"

"I don't know," Simmons said.

"Turn back."

Simmons ignored his demands and speeded down river. "Nelles, Curtis, pack the gear."

"What gear?" Eddy asked. "The last time you had them pack gear it was a trunk full of parachutes. What now?"

Simmons fiddled with the boat's gas gauge. "Rocket launchers."

"What? You have anti-aircraft weapons?"

"I knew it might eventually come down to this," Simmons said. "If we want to have any chance of getting off this river alive to blackmail them, we need a safe exit."

McKnight was yelling to Strickland over the roar of the chopper blades, "I want the woman and boys off that vessel!"

"They're my bait," Strickland said.

"Not anymore," she said, pointing her gun down on him. "Give them to me."

She fired a warning shot that ricocheted near Strickland. He backed away in the wind and motioned to one of his men, who ran below deck and returned with Mrs. Osland and her two sons. The pilot steadied the chopper as best he could while they glided downriver. Strickland and another NSA agent helped lift the family into the chopper.

"You're wasting our time," Strickland said.

She looked at Mrs. Osland who appeared tired but unharmed. The boys were wide-eyed, admiring the sharpshooter with the gun.

"You're safe now," McKnight said to the woman. "We'll take you ashore."

Mrs. Osland smiled. "Thank you."

The helicopter lifted away from the boat and flew upriver where the NSA and other military personnel had set up camp. McKnight kept looking back at Strickland's boat as it faded into the fog. She knew Strickland was heading for the houseboat.

When the chopper landed, McKnight called to one of the military police. "Take them to the tent for a debriefing. I don't want any reporters talking to them."

Curtis had unloaded wooden crates of what looked to Eddy like ammunition and Nelles assembled the rocket launchers on the boat's stern.

"What do you think, Eddy?" Alex asked.

"It's insane. My wife and kids are on that boat."

"Nobody will get hurt," Simmons said, mixing a chemical paste in a bucket. "I'm going to slow them down, that's all."

"Yeah, blow them out of the water. That'll slow them down," Eddy said.

Simmons licked his finger and tested the breeze. "No, I have a safer way. I'll make it rain."

"How?"

"This is carbon dust or what we used to call Olive Oil," Simmons said. "When you shoot it into the air above a large body of water like a river, it acts like a black tar roof. It absorbs heat and evaporation increases from the river below. Suddenly we got ourselves rain. It's not high-tech anymore, but it's reliable."

Eddy watched the tugboat closing the gap, bouncing over the wake like a large frog jumping over rocks in a stream. There were two men on the bow of the boat with rifles. Strickland spoke into a bullhorn. "Pull over."

Nelles gunned the throttle and the houseboat plowed through the water.

Simmons launched his homemade rocket straight up and it exploded in the fog above them. "This takes a few minutes. Give them a warning shot. Dispara, Curtis."

Curtis loaded one of the rocket launchers, set his aim high and let go. The missiles burned a smoky trail in the sky before exploding behind the tugboat.

The tugboat swerved but kept after them.

Curtis launched two more rockets, laughing as he let go. The explosions echoed off the bluffs.

"That's enough," Eddy said.

The engine on the houseboat chugged and choked a few times and then Eddy heard Simmons swear as he ran up to the helm. Eddy looked to Sarah, Alex, and Jason.

"What's wrong?" he asked.

"We're out of gas," Simmons said.

"What about a reserve tank?" Alex asked.

"I don't carry one," Simmons said.

The houseboat drifted in the swirling current, rotating slowly so the stern was now downriver. Nelles and Curtis lifted the heavy rocket launchers to the rooftop.

"How many shells do we have?" Simmons asked.

Curtis counted them. "Uno, dos, tres, quatro, cinco, seis. Six."

"That's it? Just six?" Waverly asked.

"I stole them," Simmons said. "You take what you can get."

"What do think they're doing?" Manning asked Strickland.

He raised his binoculars and studied the houseboat adrift. "They're waiting for us. Could be an ambush."

"We can't get any closer," Manning said. "Not with those damn missiles."

"Continue," Strickland said to the man at the helm.

"Do you have a death wish?" Manning asked.

Strickland kept eyeing the houseboat with his binoculars. "Those rocket launchers aren't very accurate."

"They don't have to be," Manning said. "We're a pretty big fucking target."

A drop of rain hit the deck, then another and another. Strickland held out his hand and looked up into the sky. A deluge of rain broke free from the clouds and fell upon the tugboat and the surrounding river. The sheets of rain were so heavy that Strickland's clothing was soaked instantly.

He removed the SAT phone from his belt as he and Manning ran for cover under the boat's awning. "Why is it raining?"

Manning shook the rain out of his short crop of hair. "I don't know. You requested fog, right?"

Strickland speed-dialed the Weather Program's command center.

"Private Holden."

"Holden, this is Craig Strickland. What the hell are you doing in the Midwest?"

"Fog, Sir." He could barely hear the Private over the roar of pounding rain.

"Check again."

"Must be some kind of mistake. You have rain there, Sir?"

"Yes, and plenty of it."

"I don't know where it's coming from," Private Holden said.

"Make it stop."

"I'm working on it. You might have to ride that storm out."

Strickland clipped the SAT phone to his belt and yelled to the agent steering the boat. "Continue on downriver."

"Here they come," Curtis yelled into the rain at Simmons. The houseboat continued its clockwise rotation in the swirling river.

"Fire," Simmons said.

Curtis launched a rocket with a high arc but it didn't explode. It just splashed in the water behind the tugboat like a skipping rock.

"A frickin' dud," Curtis said. He launched another out of frustration and it too skipped across the wake before sinking. "This ammo sucks!"

The tugboat cautiously swerved back and forth across the river toward them.

"Nelles, show them what we got," Simmons said.

Nelles spun the launcher as the houseboat twirled in the wake and the rocket speeded upward but nowhere near the tugboat.

"This is ridiculous," Eddy said. "You can't possibly aim while we're spinning like this. You'll kill my family."

Simmons spit into the rain. "Hey, we're trying to survive here, alright? What do you want us to do, jump ship?"

"That's not a bad idea," Eddy said.

Sarah looked at him curiously. "What? Jump into the river?"

Eddy didn't explain. He pushed by Jason and Alex and ran into the cabin. He grabbed the almanac, stuffing it back into the Ziploc bag he'd used to store it in the freezer at home. On top of the refrigerator was a pistol that he shoved in his pants. Back on deck he strapped on a life jacket and held the almanac up for the group.

"This is what they want, right?"

"Eddy no, don't do it," Sarah said. "It's too dangerous."

"I don't have any choice," he said. "My family is on that boat."

"They'll kill you, newspaper man," Simmons said.

"I'll distract them," Eddy said. "You get Alex ashore so he can get the video to Tom back at CNN."

Without waiting for their feedback, Eddy jumped into the wall of rain and brown water with the almanac. The river was cold and he bobbed along with droplets bouncing all around. The tugboat surged up behind him.

At first, Strickland thought they'd thrown excess cargo off the boat until he realized it was a man floating in the river. "Slow up, it's Osland."

· They pulled alongside of him, and with Manning's help, Strickland reached out his arm and hoisted Osland onto the tugboat. He stood there dripping like a wet dog.

"You finally came to your senses," Strickland said.

"Where's my family?"

Strickland saw him holding something in a plastic bag. "Is that the almanac?"

Eddy removed a gun from his dripping pants and pointed it at Strickland. "You'll get it when I get my family."

McKnight finally had the family safe inside the military tent and ran back to the helicopter to track down the tugboat. This time she didn't need her gun drawn to get them to listen to her orders.

"Over there," she said, pointing at the tugboat below.

The chopper circled the boat twice and it lowered close to the deck. McKnight could see Strickland talking to a man in a lifejacket. She recognized

Eddy Osland from photos she had seen of him on the news. She could see they were arguing with each other.

"How much closer can you get?" she asked.

"Maybe five feet. The wind and rain have picked up," the pilot said.

"You can shoot from here, can't you?" she asked the sharpshooter. He nodded. "Definitely."

"Shoot the one with the almanac."

The sharpshooter hesitated for a moment. "Pardon?"

"I said shoot that man," she demanded. "Kill him."

"But I thought-"

McKnight was losing her cool. She was tired of people questioning her orders. "I'm authorizing you to implement a one-eighty, soldier. Shoot to kill!"

The sharpshooter leveled his rifle, pointing down at the boat.

Eddy shielded his face from the chopper's wind, keeping his pistol at Strickland's head.

On the boat deck, three other NSA agents had their guns pointed at Eddy. He was at a standoff.

"Where are they? Let me see them!" Eddy said.

He looked up at the chopper hovering. A soldier above had a rifled pointed down at him as well.

"Give it up," Strickland said, smiling at him before removing the almanac from his hand.

Suddenly a bullet hit Strickland in the chest. A red stain emerged on his rain-soaked shirt. Eddy stood there, frozen in confusion, wondering if they'd hit the wrong man. The chopper lowered in the rain and the soldier fired again. Strickland buckled at the knees, dropping the almanac in the river.

Over an intercom, Eddy heard a woman in the chopper yelling to the NSA agents on the boat. "One-eighty! One-eighty!"

The three agents opened fire on Strickland ripping his body with bullets as Eddy dropped his own gun and crawled across the deck in the rain. He realized "one-eighty" meant they'd turned on one of their own. They were taking Strickland down.

Eddy looked at the Strickland sprawled out on the deck in a puddle of blood. He then looked over the edge of the boat for the almanac but it was gone. The swirling wake had taken it under.

One of the NSA agents walked over to Eddy and reached out his hand to help him up. "I'm Roy Manning. Sorry you had to see that, Mr. Osland."

Eddy stood up, with the wind and rain still blowing in his face.

"You okay?" Manning asked.

"Where's my wife and sons?"

Simmons could see they were drifting right into the government's hands and there wasn't anything he could do about it.

"Freeze!"

A team of military commandos had been perched on a train bridge above the river. As the houseboat floated by in the rain, they repelled down like spiders off a Web, while a team above held machine guns pointed at him and his crew.

"Hands above your heads," a soldier said.

"It's over," Simmons said, raising. "Ditch the rockets."

Curtis kicked the rocket launcher and remaining shells off the roof of the boat into the river. Nelles did the same with his hands raised in the air.

Simmons couldn't see the tugboat anymore and he wondered what had happened up river. Had they caught Eddy and killed him? Had years of hiding on a boat come down to this?

The commandos were storming the boat, rustling Sarah, Alex, and Jason out into the rain.

"We have a camera on board," one of them shouted.

"Take it," his commanding officer said, as he handcuffed Simmons.

The soldier yanked the camera from Jason's hands and Simmons could see the pained look on Alex's face. He'd been so close to the story and now it had been taken from him.

They escorted Eddy by a crowd of reporters and onlookers to an Army tent on the riverbank. The military police kept pushing the mass of people back, widening the perimeter with barricades. Eddy knew what it was like to be on that side of the fence, struggling for position to get a good photo or soundbite. He felt awkward as the center of everyone else's story.

A young petite woman approached him as he entered the tent. He had seen her from the boat. She'd called out the "one-eighty" before they'd gunned Strickland down.

"I'm Candace McKnight. I work with the National Security Agency," she said. "Have a seat."

The tent had nothing but a long table and folding chairs. He didn't feel like sitting. "Where's my family?"

"We have them. Ann and the boys are safe," she said. "I want you to know that we don't normally operate this way. Taking your family was Mr. Strickland's idea, not ours."

"That's it? That's your apology?"

"I'm sorry for everything that's happened to you," McKnight said.

Eddy just wanted to get out of there. "Great. Apology accepted. Where are they?"

"We have a few details we need to clear up first."

"If this is about the almanac, it's gone," Eddy said. "Strickland dropped it in the river."

"This is no longer about the almanac, Eddy," she said. "It's about the videotape and the eyewitness accounts."

The flap from the back of the tent opened and Eddy watched as Simmons, Sarah, Alex, Jason, Nelles, and Curtis were paraded inside. They were all rain-soaked, and handcuffed.

"Remove the cuffs," McKnight said to the military police officer. "Everyone take a seat."

Eddy and the group sat at the table across from McKnight. She reintroduced herself to the group and directed her first question at Eddy.

"What you did out on that river was dangerous," she said. "Are you aware that you could go to prison for risking national security?"

He was shocked at her tone of voice. "Screw your national security. Does the government alter the global weather system because it's in the best interest of its citizens?" Eddy asked. "Does murdering a government scientist, and a farm family somehow, in your grand scheme of things, protect national security?"

The tent was silent except for the sound of the wind slapping the sides. From the look on McKnight's face, Eddy knew that his outburst irritated her.

"That's quite a list of accusations," she said.

"They're all true," Eddy fired back. "I can prove everything."

McKnight smiled as she opened her briefcase on the table. She slipped on a pair of trendy red glasses. "I'd like to hear how you plan to do that."

"You killed Robert's son. You blasted him with a radio wave from a coil," Eddy said.

"A coil? Really?" McKnight said.

"Tesla's Coil," Simmons said. "The government has been researching with it for years. We saw how it works. We have it on videotape. You used your satellite to locate him and the coil killed him."

"The kid was a wreck," Eddy said. "Whatever killed him was-"

"Lightning," she said. She removed a file from her briefcase.

"Wasn't lightning." Eddy said. "I was at the autopsy. I saw Mick, and I spoke to the coroner."

"And the coroner, Dr. Neal Fischer, listed cardiac arrest as the cause of death, brought on by a lightning strike," McKnight said. She pushed a copy of the autopsy report across the table to Eddy.

Eddy remembered that two agents had watched Fischer perform the original autopsy. They must've taken a copy of the report.

"Fischer didn't believe it was lightning," Eddy said. "He wrote that because your men pressured him to."

"No notes on the report expressed any doubts," McKnight said, forcing her red glasses high on the bridge of her nose. "We can't go around questioning autopsy reports."

"You murdered that entire family," Eddy said.

"The Jacobsens?" she asked. "Fire Marshall said it was a gas explosion." She handed Eddy another report.

"Stop playing games with us," he said.

"I'm not playing games, Mr. Osland. You're making serious accusations against the United States government. Weather tampering has been a part of urban folklore for years, but it's a myth. That's all. We can't have you running around making claims of conspiracy without demonstrable proof."

"We have evidence," Waverly said. "Mick Jacobsen had an almanac where he kept records of the weather patterns."

"We could tell you what the weather will be six months from now," Simmons said. "The almanac is all the evidence we need."

Eddy stopped them. "No, it's lost. The almanac fell in the river."

"What about Dr. Kemper?" Simmons asked.

"Kemper died in a car accident," McKnight said. She searched her briefcase for another document.

"This is bullshit," Eddy said. He was frustrated at how she explained everything away in easy sound bites. "What do you want from us?"

"We're keeping the videotape. One of my men died because of all this."

"You killed him," Eddy said.

"We did what was necessary to bring it to an end," she said. "Eddy, I'm prepared to give you your life back. The murder charges will be dropped, you will be exonerated, and you'll get your family back as long as you agree to not publicize what you've seen."

He didn't like the offer. Eddy turned to his friends.

Alex surprised him by speaking up first. "Go ahead, Eddy. Take the deal."

"But this story can't go untold."

Alex smiled, shaking his head. "A lot of stories go untold, Ozzie. Don't play the martyr on this one."

"Without the almanac or the video it's our word against theirs," Jason said. "The media would need more proof."

Eddy looked over at Curtis and Nelles sitting sheepishly like students in the back of the class. "What do you two think?"

"Can't fight the machine, man," Curtis said.

Nelles nodded along with his friend. "Machine always wins."

"This is how it works," Simmons said. "Believe me, I've sat here before."

Eddy looked over at Dr. Waverly.

"I think they owe you more than your family and your reputation," she said.

She was right. He decided to use the story as his last pawn. "If we walk away from this without saying anything, I get my family and my life back. You also owe these people something."

"But we're not admitting-"

"That's the whole point, isn't it?" Eddy said, raising his voice. "You're not admitting anything. If you want the story left untold, you'll have to pay for the silence."

"What can I do?" McKnight conceded.

"Give Joe Simmons his freedom," Eddy said.

"Your freedom?" she asked.

"I've been dodging the government for years," Simmons said. "Take the Shaman off the blacklist."

McKnight continued scratching notes on her pad. "As of today, nobody in our department has ever heard of Joseph Simmons. Consider yourself a free man."

"Sarah?" Eddy asked.

She cleared her throat. "I'd like a security clearance to read the government's weather-related files."

"I don't know if I can do that," McKnight said, tapping her pen.

"I suggest you write this down," Sarah said coldly. "I'll speak slowly so you don't miss a word. Solar maximum can render a satellite useless, and if the government is relying on satellites to manipulate the world's weather, we've got a problem."

"She's right," Simmons said. "In the next few years we'll see a lot more solar activity. Solar maximum can interfere with satellites. And a dead satellite could mean unexpected changes in the weather if you're relying on the satellites to fine tune what you're doing with the coil."

"Abrupt shifts in weather can harm or even wipe out entire species of plants and animals," Waverly said. "I've already seen deformed frogs here in Minnesota."

McKnight finished writing, took off her glasses, and rubbed her eyes. "A security clearance can take up to six months to process."

"I've done work with the government," Waverly said. "You could process the papers within a week."

McKnight placed her glasses back on her pointed nose. "Anything else?"

Alex and Jason shook their heads.

Eddy looked over at his two Cuban friends. "Nelles? Curtis?"

Neither one of them said anything. They sat there silently as if they no longer understood English. Eddy figured the military presence had them spooked.

"How about citizenship? You hombres want to be Americans?" Simmons asked.

"Sí, yes," Nelles said, nodding to his friend.

McKnight sighed and wrote that down, too.

Curtis raised his skinny tattooed arm. "When we become American can Nelles and I get one of them government prescriptions for marijuana?"

"I don't think so," McKnight said.

Curtis punched Nelles. "¡Ah! Tú eres un soplatubos."

"That leaves just you, Eddy. Can you walk away from this?" McKnight asked.

He didn't want to, in fact, he hated to walk away from such an important story. "I want my wife and kids."

Candace McKnight stood up and left the tent.

A moment later Eddy heard a squealing of laughter that he hadn't heard in days. The tent flap blew open.

"Daddy!"

In a burst of excitement and joy, he reached down and scooped them up, hugging his boys.

"Mikey! Matt! Oh my, god!" he said, kissing them both. "Are you okay?" he asked, looking them over. They seemed to be in perfect health and in good spirits.

Ann stepped into the tent and Eddy handed his boys to Curtis.

"Are you hurt?" Eddy asked, looking her over. He had almost forgotten how beautiful she was.

"I'm a little shaken," she said.

"I love you, you know that?" he asked with his hands around Ann's waist.

Her eyes sparkled through the tears. "I love you, too."

"Mr. Osland there's still one minor detail I'd like to clear up, if I may," McKnight said. "A sum of forty million dollars was deposited into your bank account. And since I've given you everything you need, I was assuming we could get that money back. However, as of an hour ago we noticed you made a withdrawal of the entire sum."

Simmons smiled and whispered. "Curtis hacked his way into the bank and retrieved your PIN number. We transferred the money to a more secure offshore account. Don't give it back, newspaper man."

"I see you're still up to your old handiwork, Mr. Simmons," McKnight said, drumming her fingers on the table.

"What if I had another copy of the almanac?" Eddy asked McKnight. "How much would you pay to make sure it never surfaced? Forty million?"

"You have another copy?" she asked.

"Maybe, I can't remember," he said rubbing the cut on his forehead. "I took a hard blow to the head earlier this week."

"And a sum of forty million would help to maintain your amnesia?"

"I think so."

"Very well," McKnight said. "We'll consider the forty million a fee for contractor services. You helped the NSA find a security breach and we've paid you for your services. I don't want to hear a word about this in the press. People from my department will contact you to coach you on what you can say to the media."

Eddy kept thinking about the files he had in Maui. "Agreed."

McKnight locked her briefcase. "Good day, everyone," she said with a forced smile. "The military police will take you home. We'll be in touch."

Eddy had spent twenty minutes introducing Ann to everyone and explaining the events that had happened after Ann and the boys disappeared.

Simmons pulled his thick hair back and approached Eddy shaking his hand. "Of all the reporters that hunted me down," Simmons said, "You're the only one I ever wanted to thank."

"What will you do now, Eddy?" Waverly asked.

Eddy looked at his wife. For the first time in his life, he really had no plan, no deadline to worry about. His life was wide open. "I'll take some time off with my family," Eddy said. "Maybe go on a vacation."

Dr. Waverly reached out her arms and gave Eddy a hug. "No matter what McKnight says, you're right about this, Eddy. As I learn more, I'll call you."

Jason shook his hand. "It was a blast while it lasted."

"Just like old times, Ozzie. We have to do this again." Alex patted him on the back.

Eddy held his wife in his arms, thankful that she and the boys were safe.

"You want to go home and lay in bed for few hours?" Ann whispered.

Eddy remembered how the FBI had tore apart their home. "I have a better idea. I know of a quaint bed & breakfast that will offer us more privacy."

"Sounds wonderful," she said.

He was so full of ideas that he had thought about since Ann had left. "You know, we could plan a vacation with the kids. Get away from it all. We could rent a cabin up north."

"No cabins, Eddy. I think the boys and I have had our fill of camping for a while."

Michael and Matthew were on the floor of the tent wrestling with Curtis and Nelles. Ann seemed repulsed by their tattoos.

"Who are those two?" she asked

"A couple of friends I picked up along the way," Eddy said.

CONCLUSION

Red skies at night, sailor's delight.

THE PALM TREES swayed in the evening breeze above Eddy's head as he stared up at the clear red sky. His sons were on the beach collecting seashells and dodging white foamy surf.

The sound of "Jingle Bells" echoed from inside the small condominium. Eddy reflected on how surreal Christmas seemed without any snow or windchill. In the last few weeks, he'd grown restless and eager to get back to some constructive work, but the government-funded vacation in Maui felt pretty good.

Ann answered the ringing phone, and he listened to her hushed voice across the screened-in porch. When she stepped out into the sun, he could tell it was another call from home.

"Eddy, it's for you," she said, rolling her eyes. "It's Mark again."

Eddy sat up, wiping the suntan lotion off his hands onto his bathing suit. "Mark, what's up?"

"Ed, when will you and Ann get off that beach?"

"Soon. We'll be heading back next week," Eddy said. "The publicity has finally died down."

"It ain't right celebrating Christmas without snow. It must drive you out of your mind."

"I don't know," Eddy said, watching the red sun drop into the dark ocean like a glazed red doughnut into coffee. "It's not so bad."

"I got my icehouse out on the lake here," Mark said proudly. "Fishing isn't too bad, you know."

"Where do you have her planted?" Eddy asked, envisioning a frozen Lake Minnetonka with its icehouse villages.

"In the middle of Gideon's Bay. There's good bass out there, Ed."

"We'll be back after the holidays."

"Hey, I wanted you to know Alex Andrews called a couple of times looking for you," Mark said. "He's freelancing for CNN and he's was wondering if you had any background on the weather tampering."

Alex must've teamed up with Eddy's friend Tom DeVaney. The lure of a good story was hard for any reporter to resist.

"I'm still undecided about whether to go public with this or not," Eddy said, walking into a small study where he kept his computer and files. On the desk were newspaper clippings about the lunatic, Craig Strickland that had allegedly kidnapped Eddy's family before he was gunned down. The FBI had made Eddy seem like a hero in the press for helping authorities solve the case. He felt guilty about how the NSA had pinned everything on one man.

He used his foot to lift the top off a Kinko's box that contained the only surviving copy of the almanac.

"I'm fishing this weekend. What's the weather forecast in that almanac?"

Eddy flipped ahead to December, reading Mick Jacobsen's handwriting. "Saturday's supposed to be light snow, and then you'll have about six or seven inches on Sunday."

"Thanks, buddy. The wife's calling me to bed. Merry Christmas. See you next week."

"Merry Christmas to you too, Mark."

Eddy hung up the phone and continued reading December's forecasts in the almanac. The month would be hit hard by four storms amounting to over three feet of snow. He walked back into the living room where Ann was watching the boys through the window.

"What did Mark say?" she asked.

"The usual. He called to tell me we should go back to Minnesota. And Alex has been looking for me as well," he said, sparing his wife the details.

THE DEAD FARMER'S ALMANAC

"Alex? Why is he looking for you?"

"He needs background information for a story," Eddy said, picking up the television remote, tuning to the Weather Channel. A colorful weather map of the mainland showed snow over Minnesota. The estimated snowfall for Sunday was six inches, just as Mick had predicted months ago.

He could feel his wife watching him from across the room. "Eddy, what are you doing?"

"I'm checking the weather back home," he answered, comparing the weather map on TV to Mick's almanac.

"Is the almanac still accurate?"

He knew she was watching him closely. "Sure is."

"What are you planning to do about it?" she asked, folding her arms.

He was tempted to go public with the story but even with the almanac, it would be hard to prove. A lot of skeptics out there would shoot holes in a story like this. "I don't know yet."

He could feel the heat of his wife's stare. He knew his interest in the story upset her. "So help me, Edward Anthony Osland. You promised no investigative stories until after the Holidays. Please turn the TV off."

Listen to her, he reminded himself. You promised not to work on vacation.

Her tone grew louder. "Eddy, please turn that TV off."

And he did.